Seizing Justice

Stephanie Tennile

I Dedicate...

This book is dedicated to life. Working on this rewrite helped me find peace, balance, self, love, and all that is important in LIFE.

To the Readers

Thank you for taking this journey with Justice and those she holds dear. I appreciate your love and support of not just my characters but of me as well. Now…

Seizing Justice

Stephanie Tennile

Chapter 1

Justice's Suite

The sun shone through the floor-to-ceiling windows of the Omni hotel in San Diego. It was a beautiful summer day in June. A breeze was blowing in the Gaslamp Quarter off the San Diego Bay, making it just the perfect temperature for a summer wedding. Justice loved the water, she loved the beach, so a summer wedding near the ocean wasn't a stretch.

    Justice Rashé was finally getting married, or at least that was the way her mother, Leslie, and her friends felt. She was excited her wedding day was finally here, but she knew with her schedule and Taryll Johnson, her fiancée's, schedule they were going to have a lot of work waiting for them once this was all over and done with.

    Justice owned two dance studios and small movie lot where her company, Just Breath & Dance Incorporated, filmed music videos for different artists and groups in Los Angeles and Malibu. Prior to her wedding, she had acquired another dance studio in San Francisco and was now in the process of hiring someone in the Bay area to run the day to day so she wouldn't have to travel back and forth so much.

    Saying they were constantly busy, and travelling was an understatement, but Justice wouldn't have it any other way. Their love of music was one of the many things she and Taryll shared; and now they were going to share their lives together. Our love for music may be an easier thing to share, she thought as she starred at her dress.

Justice adjusted the earbuds in her ears and turned up the volume on her cellphone. She was listening to Damien Escobar. She loved his music, he played the violin, it always soothed her when she was stressed, and boy was she stressed.

Justice had woken up earlier than she had set her alarm for. She was up before the sun, since about four a.m. sitting at the end of the bed, listening to Damien Escobar, Lucine Fyelon, Duke Ellington, John Coltrane, and Najee; starring at the wedding dress hanging on the back of the door.

A million and one thoughts, questions, and doubts running through her head, that even the music couldn't quiet. *I don't know how to be a wife, what if he realizes I am not the woman he wants, what if he leaves, what if I mess up, what if, what if, what if.* She sat on the end of the king-sized bed starring at the beautiful cream-colored mermaid cut gown, she hit repeat on Damien Escobar's *A Winter Night in Boston*.

What Justice loved most about her dress was the almost five-foot-long train of her wedding dress. A part of her couldn't believe the day had finally come, mostly because she and Taryll had changed the date three times before handing all control over to their mothers. Had it been left to them they still would have been saying they were too busy to get married. At one point they had decided they would just go to the Los Angeles courthouse and get married, but their mothers wouldn't have heard of such nonsense.

Not able to handle the tasks of planning a wedding or trusting a wedding planner to do so with so little input on their parts, they decided they would leave the planning to their mothers, and their mothers had gone all out. Everything seemed big and over the top to

Justice, but her mother was happy, and that made her happy. Her brother Justin's death nine years ago, cheated her mother out of marrying her brother and his girlfriend at the time, Katherine Whitmore, whom everyone called Katie.

Justice got up from her seat at the end of the bed and went over to sit at the vanity. She needed to get moving. She took her earbuds out and turned the volume up on her cellphone, sitting it on the vanity.

She would have to head to the church in the next hour and she didn't want to be late. As she started to apply her lipliner she noticed her hands were shaking. Justice put the lipliner down on the table and stood up. She shook her hands out and took a deep breath holding it for a few seconds then let it out. You're alright, she thought, you've got this.

Justice sat back down at the vanity and with shaking hands started to apply the lipliner, only to wipe it off and start again, then to wipe it off again. She dropped the liner on the tabletop again and sighed. What is wrong with me she thought. The man she was marrying was the same man she had been with for the past eleven years. They had been dating since she was sixteen, and now at twenty-seven they were finally tying the knot.

What if I am not a good wife? She thought. Justice sighed as she looked at her reflection in the mirror. She could see the anxiety in her light brown eyes, and she wanted to cry. Why am I freaking out, she thought, and then there was a knock on the door?

Kayla Jones let herself in after there wasn't answer from Justice. Kayla looked stunning in her aqua colored halter floor length chiffon dress. The dress was cut low in the front bringing attention to her breast, and it was cut low in the back showing off her toned shoulders and back. She looked as though she stepped right off the pages of a bridal magazine.

She watched for a second as Justice hung her head. Kayla and Justice had been best friends since they were old enough to walk. Kayla had been with Justice through the loss of her father, her brother, and her mother's horrible second marriage. To say they knew each other better than they knew their selves was an understatement. So, Kayla knew her girl, her sister from another mother, was anxious, scared, nervous, excited, and petrified the moment she walked in the door. Kayla walked over to the vanity and bent down to face Justice.

"Sweetie." She called. Justice looked up and gave a half smile.

"You could do your makeup in your sleep." Kayla teased. Kayla knew her friend so well. She had been with Taryll and Justice since they first started dating, hell she had been there when they were all kids and Justice used to beg her brother if she could hang out with him and Taryll. Justice's older brother, Justin, and Taryll were best friends growing up. Kayla thought about Justin and knew just as she did, Justice had to be missing his presence, Justin died the summer before their senior year in high school.

"I'm nervous Kay. I know Taryll and I have been together almost twelve years and it's time we get married, but I'm just not sure I can be the wife he needs. Hell, I don't know how to be a wife at all. What does that even look like?" Justice rambled on.

Kayla laughed, which got the attention of the other women in the living room of the suite. Monique Rogers, Tasha Martin-Williams, and Zaria Morales were Justice's bridesmaids. They came in the bedroom where Kayla was now applying Justice's makeup.

"What is she over here complaining and whining about now?" Monique asked, as she ran her hands down the front of her aqua colored off the shoulder tea length chiffon and lace bridesmaid dress. The dress accented her long legs, at five foot seven without heels, she was all legs, and the dress fit her perfectly. Monique was Justice's friend from high school. Monique was the one Justice would get into trouble, so to speak, with. She introduced Justice to her first club, her first drink, and was there to hold her hair when it all came back up.

Justice rolled her eyes and looked in the mirror, Kayla had fixed her makeup and for that she was grateful. If it were left to her, she would still be in the mirror trying to fix it this time tomorrow.

"I'm not complaining; I just don't know if I can be the wife he needs." Tasha looked at Justice and smiled. Tasha was wearing an aqua A-line crinkle sweetheart floor length chiffon dress. The dress accentuated her large breasts and broad shoulders.

Tasha was the only one in their group who was already married. She met her husband, Christopher Williams, her first year at Grambling State University, and knew he was going to be her husband. They were inseparable, and within months after their graduation they were married.

"Justice, you and Taryll have been together for eleven years, and yes, I understand part of that you were in high school, part of it was spent as a long-distance relationship, but you have survived all of that and you have made it to your wedding day. You have been all the woman that man has needed all these years and trust me that isn't going to change just because you become Mrs. Taryll Johnson. You will be a great wife; you need not worry about that. Trust me if you have any questions, you both can call Chris and I; Lord knows that we have had our ups and downs, but we made it." Tasha said as she hugged her best friend. Justice smiled and blew out the breath she was holding. She could do this, I can do this, she thought.

Chapter 2

Taryll's Suite

Taryll Johnson stood on the balcony of his suite, looking out at the San Diego Bay. It was a beautiful site, he could stand here all day, but he knew that couldn't happen. In his suite his best man and groomsmen were getting dressed and conversating. The weather was almost perfect for a Saturday in late June, not too hot. He took a sip of water from the glass he was holding and let out a sigh.

Taryll was a music producer and owned his own label, with studios in New York City and Los Angeles. He and his business partner, Ryan Cox, just opened another studio in Atlanta about six months ago. As he thought of all the things he and Justice had going on, all the balls in the air as it were, he realized there was so much that needed to be done outside of this wedding and their honeymoon.

How has this wedding been blown up to be such a big affair? What am I doing? I love her, no question, but can I be the husband she needs? The husband she deserves. Will I screw this up, just like my dad, he thought?

Everyone he knew was going to be in attendance, as well as some of the artists and groups he and Justice had worked with over the years. Heck, his mother had even gotten Paul Taylor to play at their reception. How she pulled that off he'd never know, because he wasn't an artist he or Justice had ever worked with, but she knew he was one of Justice's favorite jazz artists.

The last time he had spoken to his mother and his soon to be mother-in-law the guest list consisted of almost two hundred people, he could only imagine what the count was now. Taryll wished he and Justice had just gone to the courthouse and taken care of this, but he knew his mother would take him just to the edge of death then tap in Justice's mother to finish him off.

His mother, Angela, and Justice's mother, Leslie, were best friends, and had been since college. They both attended USC for undergrad, then his mother went off to med school and Leslie went off to law school. He knew his mother would do anything to see Leslie as happy as she was today, and if that meant she would help put together a larger-than-life wedding for her now only child, then that was what she would do.

Taryll took another sip from his glass and wished it was something stronger, way stronger than the water with lemon he was nursing. He wasn't having second thoughts it was just the nagging thoughts he had his entire life that were bothering him now. Was he going to be like his father?

Stephanie Tennile

Chapter 3
Two Years Earlier

Taryll sat at the table in his mother's kitchen finishing his second cup of coffee. He was certain he wanted to marry Justice and he wanted to spend the rest of his life with her, but he didn't know if he could be the husband she needed. He had been thinking about proposing for months, he had even bought a ring, but never asked the question.

Angela walked into the kitchen and to the refrigerator. She loved when her son was home, which wasn't often enough for her. Although he lived in California, he might as well live on the moon because she hardly ever saw him.

She planned to make Taryll his favorite dinner before he disappeared yet again. It seemed her youngest son was constantly on the go. She didn't get to see him as often as she would like. Taryll graduated high school valedictorian and got accepted to Rutgers University in New Jersey, Cornell University in New York, UCLA, USC, Tulane University in Louisiana, and the University of New Orleans. Angela was so proud of all the acceptance letters he had received, but silently prayed he would stay close to home and go to USC or UCLA, but he accepted the scholarship to Tulane University in New Orleans Louisiana.

Taryll had attended Tulane for his freshman and sophomore years, then transferred to UCLA at the beginning of his junior year. He wanted to be closer to Justice after her brother died and she was in a bad car accident herself. Once he graduated from UCLA, he moved to New York to get is master's in business from NYU. Once he graduated grad school, he moved back to California, opened his first recording studio and bought his house in Malibu.

"Mom, what do you think of Justice?" Taryll asked as he got up to put his coffee cup in the sink. He rolled his eyes as soon as the question came out of his mouth. He knew she loved her. He knew she was crazy about Justice ever since she was a little girl, hell his mom was at the hospital after she was born, and she was her godmother. She would spoil her as a little kid because she had always wanted a girl, but instead had two boys before she and his father had divorced.

"I love Justice, you know that, why?" She asked, already knowing the answer, and it's about time she thought. Angela pulled the chicken out the refrigerator and placed the bowl on the counter. She had the chicken sitting in a buttermilk marinade over night. She pulled out a large skillet and poured in a little oil and turned the fire up under the pan.

"I want to ask Justice to marry me Ma." Taryll said as he leaned against the counter and watch his mother move around the kitchen preparing his favorite smothered chicken with portabella mushrooms and onions.

"Well son, all I can say is, it's about time you took this step. You two aren't getting any younger and all of this playing house isn't good for either of you." Angela said as she wiped her hands on the towel in the pocket of her apron. She started to cut up the mushrooms.

"Mom, what are you talking about... we aren't playing house." Taryll answered almost too quickly.

Stephanie Tennile

He knew how his mother felt about him and Justice being intimate prior to marriage. She wasn't happy when he and Justice had lived together her senior year of high school, but that was the last time they had lived together. After she graduated, she moved to Orange County to attend Chapman University and he had moved back home for his last year at UCLA before moving to New York.

She placed the mushrooms in a bowl and grabbed two yellow onions. She knew the conversation wasn't going to go well with her son. She had wanted him to wait until he was married to Justice to have a physically intimate relationship with her. Angela was raised to wait until marriage, and she had raised her sons to wait as well, but she wasn't naïve, she knew that ship done sailed.

"Okay Taryll, but you know how I feel about that. But we can go ahead and drop that portion of the conversation. Yes, I love Justice, and I think it's great you are going to ask her to marry you."

"Thanks Mom." Taryll kissed his mother on the cheek. He went to the fridge and grabbed a bottle of water, grabbed his keys, and told her he would be back in time for dinner. Taryll headed to his car, and at first, he wanted to go and ask Justice at that very moment, then doubt crept in again. He headed to his brother's place.

Taryll pulled up in front of Brandon's house and his sister-in-law, Sharon, was walking out the door with

Brandon on her heels. Sharon was carrying their two-year-old son, Brandon Jr on her hip to her car.

"I'm not going to fight Brandon. I'm tired of it. All the late nights... I'm not stupid." She said as she fastened Brandon Jr into his car seat. She closed the door and crossed her arms under her chest. Brandon was now standing in front of her pleading.

"Sharon, it isn't what you think. I am just working late, there's no one else." He said. Brandon was an entertainment lawyer for a law firm in Los Angeles. He recently landed some new clients and had been working late hours and pulling a ton of overtime building client relations.

"I'll call you." Sharon said as she got in the car and drove off.

Taryll stood by his car watching the whole exchange until Brandon called his name. What the hell is going on, he thought?

"What's up T?" Brandon asked as Taryll walked toward him in the driveway. Brandon really didn't want to be bothered but he hardly saw his brother since he opened his studio and started building his recording label. He had been working non-stop to get it off the ground and to find talented artist to work with. He motioned for him to follow him into the house.

Brandon closed the door behind them and asked Taryll if he wanted a beer. Taryll nodded yes, and Brandon grabbed two Coronas from the fridge.

"So, what's going on with you and Sharon?" Taryll asked as he took a sip of his Corona. It had been a while since he had one and it felt good.

"She thinks I am cheating because of all the late hours that I've been putting in at the firm. I told her I just picked up two new clients and have been working on building a relationship with them, but she doesn't want to hear it." Brandon took a long swallow of his Corona and sat the bottle on the table.

"What would make her think you were cheating; you guys haven't had any issues." Taryll said and took another drink from his beer.

Brandon looked at the table and grabbed his beer finishing the last of what was in the bottle. Taryll knew the look on his brother's face, he messed up.

"What'd you do Brandon?" Taryll asked, but in his mind, he already knew the answer.

Brandon got up from the table, grabbed another beer, and popped it open. He hadn't told his brother about what had happened about a year ago, and he didn't want to.

"Enough about me and my marriage, what's up with you?" He sipped his beer and came back to the table.

Knowing his brother was trying to change the subject, Taryll finished off his beer and leaned back in his seat. He stared at his brother before replying. "B, I want to ask Justice to marry me."

Brandon put his beer down and smiled at his brother. He was happy for his little brother. Taryll and Justice had been together for years, and he already saw her as a little sister anyway because they had all grown up together.

"Well Tar, it's about damn time. You guys have been together longer than Sharon and I have." He laughed and took another drink of his beer. Taryll laughed but didn't say anything.

"Okay…what's bothering you T? And before you say nothing, remember, I know you. I know when something's wrong with you, when you're lying, and when you're pissed." Brandon knew his brother; something was on his mind. Taryll exhaled and replied.

"I am afraid that if I marry her, I will end up hurting her the way Dad hurt Mom. I am afraid I'll mess around and be unfaithful, and then eventually walk away, just like Dad." Taryll had never voiced his fears before, they were always thoughts that ran through his head. This wasn't the first time he wanted to ask Justice to marry him. He had thought about asking her to marry him after he had moved in with her during her senior year. He had considered buying a ring and everything but with all the doubts he had he just couldn't bring himself to do it.

Brandon could see the fear, insecurity, and the doubt in his brother's eyes, and he knew he had to tell him what happened between him and Sharon a year ago.

"Look T, only one of us can end up making the mistakes Dad did, and I already beat you to it." He said trying to lighten the mood, but it didn't.

"What?" Taryll looked up at Brandon who was now leaning against the counter in the kitchen. "When did this happen? Now? Is that why Sharon stormed out of here?"

Brandon exhaled and ran his hand through his curly hair. It was part of the reason she ran out of here because she felt they were having a repeat of what had happened a year ago.

"It was a little over a year ago. No, I take that back, it was probably about a year and a half ago because BJ was still a baby. Sharon was so wrapped up in taking care of him, I was working all the time because I just started at the firm, and I wanted to make a good impression. Anyway, when I would get home Sharon was either sleep because she had been dealing with BJ all day, or she was too tired to pay me any attention."

Brandon stopped and looked at his brother. Taryll was listening and didn't interject. He couldn't believe what his brother was telling him. Taryll knew without a doubt Brandon loved Sharon more than he loved himself and would never hurt her.

"I missed my wife T. I missed holding her, making love to her, her desiring to be with me. She was tired and overwhelmed. Brandon wasn't an easy baby, he didn't sleep through the night, and was colicky. When I would want to be intimate with her, she refused because she was tired. I'm not saying what I did was her fault, I take full responsibility, but I did what I did because I was lonely." Brandon dropped his head; he was embarrassed and ashamed of what he did.

"I started seeing a lawyer from another firm. I was working with one of her colleagues on a contract for a client when we met. At first it was innocent, we would get together for coffee, talk shop and go about our days, and then it grew into something more. Before I knew it, I was meeting her at a hotel downtown at lunch. Sharon found out when she was paying the credit card bill. She asked about the multiple charges that were made at the hotel over the course of the month and I couldn't lie to her. So, because of my selfishness a year and a half ago she has a hard time trusting me when I work late, or I have to go away for work." Brandon finished the last of his beer and put the bottle in the trash.

"Taryll, you have nothing to worry about. You're a good man. You have never stepped out on Justice… never had a desire or reason to. You're not going to end up like Dad, or me."

Taryll didn't know what to say, all he knew was he had even more doubt than before he got here. If his brother could mess up and step out on his wife, what chance did he have of doing right, he thought? Brandon could see Taryll was still struggling with the thoughts and the doubt.

"T, maybe you should talk to Pastor Tyler." Brandon said.

Chapter 4

Present Day

As if he could sense the turmoil and confusion going on in his brother's head, Brandon Johnson walked onto the balcony with two glasses of Crown Royal in his hands. Brandon was four years older than Taryll and knew his brother was dealing with something and had an idea of exactly what it was. Taryll had come to Brandon before he asked Justice to marry him with his worries about being a good husband, and not turning out like their father.

"You know little brother; you should be getting dressed, not standing out here in a pair of flannel pajama pants and a tank. This isn't exactly what Ma wants to see you in right now." Brandon said as he handed Taryll the glass.

Taryll sighed and sat his glass of water on the patio table and took a sip from the glass of Crown Royal on ice. He leaned against the balcony and ran his hands through his curly hair. His mind was racing, and he need his brother to hear him out.

"Brandon, man, my mind is reeling. I am thinking about all the work that's on my desk, contracts invoices, this wedding, and the ever-nagging thought of not doing right by J, not being the man she needs me to be." Taryll pulled a chair away from the table and sat down. Brandon did likewise and looked at his brother. He knew Taryll struggled with the same thoughts he struggled with when he had gotten married almost eight years ago.

"B, I don't know if I can be what she needs." Taryll hung his head and sighed.

"Taryll you've been what she's needed since you started dating in high school, and as you guys got older, and as your relationship evolved. You were what she needed when you were away at school, when she was always at school. So why is it going to change now that you share a last name? You two have been like a married couple for almost eleven years, it's just becoming legal man." Brandon stated with a chuckle.

"Hell, doesn't the state of California look at you all like you're married anyway?" Brandon took a sip of his drink and leaned back in the patio chair.

"What if she changes her mind and decides that being with me isn't what she wants?" Taryll asked, there he said it, but before Brandon could answer, Ryan Cox his friend and partner rushed onto the balcony.

At six foot five inches tall and almost two hundred and fifty pounds of pure muscle, you would have thought that the blonde-haired blue-eyed music executive was a pro-athlete. He was dressed in his black tux with a crisp white dress shirt, aqua blue cummerbund, and aqua blue bow tie. The blue of the tie really made his blue eyes more intense.

"Taryll, man your mother is looking for..." Before he could finish his statement, Angela Johnson walked onto the balcony. Angela was just a hair over five foot and looked more like thirty rather than her almost sixty years. She was wearing a beautiful A-line V-neck asymmetrical tulle dress with sequin beading on the cap sleeves. Her shoulder length hair was curled and pinned to the top of her head with a few curls falling at the nape of her neck.

"Taryll Greyson Johnson, you should be dressed by now. Justice is dressed and ready to go and her mother and I will not allow her to leave this hotel before you. You're supposed to be at the church waiting for her, not the other way around young man. Now get in that room and get in your tux." Angela stood her ground. She was known for being tough with her boys, ever since their father had asked for a divorce when Taryll was twelve, she was left to raise them alone.

Taryll got up from his seat, knowing his mother wasn't playing, she had thrown his middle name into the mix and that was never a good thing. He moved past his mother into the suite, kissing her on the cheek, she grabbed the glass from his hand. Taryll grabbed his tux and his shoes and headed toward the bathroom. The other guys in the suite looked at each other as Taryll locked the door behind him.

He didn't mind getting dressed in the room with his boys; he just needed a moment alone. He needed some space to think, and most of all, he needed a private moment to pray. He was still full of nerves, and although everyone was telling him this was normal, this wasn't his normal. Things didn't rattle him like this. Whatever he wanted, he went after and for the most part, he always succeeded. This was different. He felt due to the way he was raised, without a father, he would end up doing what he did.

About fifteen minutes later, Taryll walked out the bathroom dressed and ready to go. He was sure he could get through this. We have been together almost all our lives, he thought and smiled. Ryan walked over and fixed his bowtie.

Stephanie Tennile

"You alright man?" Ryan asked with concern, he had never seen his boy as nervous as he was when he went into that bathroom. Taryll was always the picture of confidence. Nothing ever seemed to get under his skin. Taryll looked at him and smiled, he was alright, well at least he hoped he was.

In the suite right above, them Justice was getting up out of the chair she was sitting in. She took a deep breath and gathered her train in her arms. And as if they were thinking the same thing, Justice and Taryll said simultaneously,

"Let's do this!"

Chapter 5
The Wedding

Getting to the church was one thing but waiting for Justice to arrive was another. He was good on the ride to the church, laughing and joking with his boys in the limo, but now sitting here and knowing Justice hadn't made it to the church yet was bringing back feelings from the hotel. As he sat in Pastor Tyler's office, he thought about how he had been sitting in this very office over a year ago spilling his guts.

As Taryll started to pace, Pastor Tyler asked the other men to give them a minute. After the men were gone Pastor Tyler stepped in front of Taryll, placed his hands on his shoulders and stopped him from pacing.

"Son, you are going to run a groove in my floor." He chuckled, remembering he had made the same comment about a few years earlier when Taryll first came to see him.

"I'm sorry." Taryll looked at the floor, stopped pacing, and sat back down and took a deep breath, then started tapping his foot. Taryll had so much energy he didn't know what to do.

"You alright Son?" Pastor Tyler asked putting his hand on Taryll's knee. Taryll looked up at Pastor Tyler and gave him half a smile. Taryll couldn't believe how much of a nervous mess he was. He had prayed before he left the hotel, he thought he was good. Then they got in the limousine and headed to the church. As soon as they arrived all the nerves were right back in the pit of his stomach.

"I am a nervous mess; this is not me. I am usually more composed than this." Taryll said as he started to tap his foot again.

"If you weren't nervous, I would think something was wrong. Every man is nervous on his wedding day."

"What if she changed her mind, what if something happened, what if..." Taryll's mind ran through almost twenty different scenarios before he could take his next breath.

"Son, that girl hasn't changed her mind, and if something happened, she would call you before she called her own mother. Everything is fine. She is just a little late that's all. Haven't you heard of fashionably late." Pastor Tyler chuckled and looked at the wall clock. Justice was only five minutes late; the way Taryll was carrying on you would have thought the girl was hours late.

"Son don't worry she will be..." Pastor Tyler started but was cut off by a knock at the door.

Leslie stuck her head in the room to let Taryll and Pastor Tyler know Justice was in place and Taryll needed to head to his spot at the altar. Pastor Tyler smiled at Taryll who had just let out the breath he seemed to be holding. Taryll started to laugh at the thoughts that were running through his mind.

He stood up and shook off all the negative thoughts, all the worries, all his fears. This is what I want, this is what she wants, he thought. He knew in his hear and in his spirit that he was doing the right thing. He knew they were meant to be together, he just had to stop letting the enemy play with his mind.

"Let's get you married." Pastor Tyler said. I am not my father, he thought as Taryll followed him out of his office, closing the door behind him and followed Pastor Tyler to the sanctuary.

The church was packed. There were chairs on the outer aisles and some people were standing in the back and in the balcony. Taryll watched as his best man and Justice's maid of honor walked down the aisle to one of as one of favorite artists, Damien Escobar, played the violin. Taryll watched as the flower girl scattered the last of her rose petals and Damien stopped playing. He looked from is goddaughter to the back of the church as the doors opened, and there she stood.

In a beautiful cream-colored mermaid cut dress, Justice stood, arm in arm with her uncle. The tension he felt melted away, the thoughts of him being a bad husband disappeared, everyone in the church disappeared, and all he could see was his beautiful bride standing at the end of the aisle.

He remembered the first time he met her; she was just a baby. He could remember when they were kids growing up, he couldn't stand her always tagging along with him and Justin. She was always getting them in trouble. Telling on them whenever they didn't include her in the games they would play. Then he remembered the day he *saw* her.

"Oh no, here she comes." Justin said to his friends, the other guys on the varsity football team, and they all chuckled. It was his senior year, and he was

Stephanie Tennile

trying to enjoy himself, but this was also Justice's freshman year. Taryll knew Justin didn't want to "babysit" his little sister. Justice had started at a different high school because her mother wanted her to attend a prestigious all girl school, but Justice didn't like the school and begged to go to high school with her brother. At the end of the first trimester her mother transferred her to the public-school Justin attended.

"Justin, Justin, I tried out for the dance team." She stated as she jumped up and down, she was so excited.

"And why are you telling me?" Justin asked turning his attention back to his friends. Justice frowned and crossed her arms over her chest. Taryll looked at her and then at Justin and frowned.

"I thought you would want to know, I made the team, and not the freshman dance team but the varsity dance team. So, I will be dancing during the halftime shows of your games." She stated with her hands on her hips. She put an emphasis on your, turned and walked away.

Taryll knew his best friend wasn't going to like the idea of being on a bus with his younger sister to all the away games, and not to mention the fact the dance team had some pretty skimpy outfits. That made Taryll a little upset, the idea of the other guys on the team and then the guys from the other schools seeing her dressed like that. *Why does that bother me, he thought, she's not my little sister.*

"Whatever." Justin said and went on talking to his friends. Taryll hit Justin in the shoulder.

"What was that for?" Justin asked rubbing his arm.

"You could have at least faked being interested in what J was saying." Taryll said as he picked up his duffle bag, Calculus book, and went after her.

Seizing Justice

"Hey, wait up J. Hold up!" He yelled out.

"What, what do you want?" Justice asked as she wiped away a tear. Taryll watched as she quickly wiped a tear from her cheek. He knew she wasn't a crier, so for her to shed a tear meant she was truly hurt by the way her bother had treated her.

"I just wanted to say congratulations. I think it's great you made the varsity team. You're a really good dancer. I remember how you use to put together routines and put on little performances when you were a kid. You have a lot of talent." Justice smiled. I don't remember her being this cute, he thought.

"Thanks Tar, I appreciate it. But you didn't have to come and say something nice because of Justin being a knucklehead... I can handle him; he'll have to watch his back when we get home." Justice laughed. He knew it was true, she would make him pay for embarrassing her the way he did.

"Well don't do anything that will get you in too much trouble, you know Winter Formal is coming up and if you get grounded who am I supposed to go with?" Taryll asked matter-of-factly, but it caught him by surprise. He saw the look of disbelief on her face and understood completely why it was there. He had never expressed any interest in her before this moment, but to be honest he had never really seen her until this moment.

"Yes, I want to go with you. Will you go with me?" He quickly added.

"I would like that." She smiled and then walked off. Taryll watched her walk away, there was something different about her. She wasn't the pestering little girl he used to hate bringing along. Was it the tone of her voice, the way she carried herself? He wasn't sure. What he was sure of though, she had him feeling a way about her *he had not felt before. Now how do I explain it to Justin, he thought.*

Justice watched her goddaughter Leilani walk very slowly down the aisle dropping the cream-colored rose petals on the floor. She was nervous, and she just couldn't put her finger on why. She loved Taryll, she couldn't remember a time when she didn't. They had been together for years, nothing was really changing she thought, or was it? Of course not, she thought, the only change will be my last name. We are still us, she thought. Her uncle Richard, her father's brother, looked at her and could see something was on her mind.

"Are you okay Jus? You're shaking." Richard asked. Justice was shaking like a leaf.

"Nervous." She said as she tapped his arm with her hand trying to regain her composure.

"You will be just fine, baby girl, just fine." Richard kissed her cheek, then led her down the aisle.

"Taryll, son, are you going to take her hand or are you just going to stare at the girl?" Pastor Tyler asked with a chuckle, as he looked from Taryll to Justice's uncle Richard who was trying to give her away. Justice smiled as Taryll blushed and took her hand. The congregation laughed. After eleven years, he still can't focus when he is in her presence, Chris Williams, thought.

"You look amazing, J." Taryll whispered to Justice as he helped her up the two steps to the podium. Justice mouthed thank you and then focused her attention on Pastor Tyler. She was trying hard not to cry. She didn't want her make-up to run and ruin her wedding photos.

"The couple decided to write their own vows so Taryll you're first." Pastor Tyler held the microphone in front of him so he wouldn't have to let go of Justice's hands.

"Sweetheart, I remember you as a little girl and how I would tell your brother to get rid of you," he chuckled as well as the congregation.

"Seeing you every day, but not really *seeing* you. Then one day, God opened my eyes. That is the only way I can explain it because I don't know what else it could have been. You were still my best friend's baby sister, but you were different. You were more than that, and over the years I've been able to see what that more was. You are sophisticated, talented, kind-hearted, loving, caring, sexy; you were the woman God had purposed to be in my life. And because He made you for me, I promise to love you, cherish you, take care of you, be there through the good and the bad, be that shoulder to cry on, the sounding board for you to toss ideas at, I am willing to be everything you need me to be and everything God needs me to be for you. I love you."

Justice had stopped breathing, and she did not even know it. She had been holding her breath for almost his entire vows, because when Pastor Tyler had informed her that it was her turn and held the microphone in front of her, she exhaled.

"I'm sorry," she said. "I didn't realize I was holding my breath." The congregation laughed. "You would think after eleven years I would know everything there is to know about this wonderful man standing before me. Wow. I thank God for you Babe. In you I have found safety here on earth. God has made you for me. I know He has because of the way we click. The way you I finish your sentences, or you can tell me exactly what it is I am going to say before I say it. The way you can read me, and the way I can read you. You are my better half, you complete me, Taryll. You are the one I can trust with whatever is on my heart. God created you for me because everywhere I am weak you are strong and, in every way, I am lacking you pick up the slack. I promise to be that for you too. I promise to tell you when you are right and when you are wrong. I promise to never hold anything back. I promise to tell you the truth even if it may hurt, I promise to be your best friend. I promise to be the helpmate you need, and God has called me to be for you. I pray God will help me to be all it is you need as a wife, a friend, a lover, a help mate. I promise to love you, cherish you, respect you, honor you, and obey. I love you."

"Will you please hand me the rings?" Pastor Tyler asked Brandon and Kayla, then handed them to Justice and Taryll.

"With these rings, you become one flesh. You are no longer two. Do you understand the commitment you are making, not only to each other but to God?"

"I do." Taryll said.

"I do." Justice stated. They placed the rings on each other's finger.

"I now pronounce you Mr. and Mrs. Taryll Greyson Johnson. You may kiss your bride." Taryll lifted the veil that covered Justice's face and saw she was crying, as he wiped away her tears he leaned in and kissed her, nothing over the top, just a nice soft kiss that gently brushed her lips. Justice opened her eyes and looked into her husband's.

"I will save the good kisses for tonight." Taryll said. Justice smiled and kissed him lightly on the cheek. She understood. They had told each other that they weren't going to have sex again until they were married, that was over four years ago. So, she could only imagine what their honeymoon was going to be like, and she was looking forward to every moment of it.

Chapter 6

Disgust

He intentionally arrived at the wedding late. He didn't want or need to be seen, at least not yet. There were so many people from his past in attendance, he was running the risk of being recognized. He hadn't seen them in years though, he had made it a point not to stay in contact. He leaned against the back wall of the church near the paparazzi and media, doing his best to look as though he belonged with them. He had brought him camera from the car when he noticed they were there. He lifted his camera and took some photos of Justice as she walked down the aisle.

He thought he was over her, he thought he had gotten her out of his system. But when he saw her again a few years ago, the feelings all came rushing back. At first, he had been upset when she hadn't recognized him, but then realized it could work to his advantage.

He had run into the grocery store just to grab a two liter of Pepsi to mix with the Jack Daniels he had at home, it had been a long day, a frustrating day. His boss was on his ass for something he didn't do, and his co-worker was taking credit for what he did. He just couldn't win. He grabbed the Pepsi from the shelf and turned to head to the register when he ran right into the woman standing beside him.

"Oh, my bad, I didn't see you." He spoke to the woman.

"No, it was my fault, I was trying to grab the Cherry Pespi near you when I should have just waited for you to move." The woman said.

"It's fine." He said and watched as the woman smiled and walked away. He knew her, he knew her voice, and he knew her walk. It was Justice Rashé. He recognized everything about her right down to the perfume she was wearing, but she hadn't recognized him. She hadn't said it was nice to see him after all these years. He started to feel hot under the collar. He was pissed.

How could she forget who I am, he thought. He headed to the front of the store near the registers hoping to get a glimpse of her again, and he had, just as she was walking out of the front doors.

He took another photo, this time of the woman he had loved all his life married the man he despised, the man who had stolen her from him.

Stephanie Tennile

He hated Taryll with a passion; and had for years. He wished he could just kill him, get him out of the way, but knew if he did, he would kill apart of Justice too, and no matter how much he hated it, he just couldn't kill him. He loved her too much to hurt her, and that would undeniably hurt her.

When he heard the announcement that Justice and Taryll were getting married, he was so mad he had to blow off some steam. He had gone to the gun range and shot every weapon he could rent, imagining the target was Taryll. When the wedding was first announced there was talk about it everywhere he went. He couldn't turn the television or radio on without hearing how "music's power couple was finally tying the knot."

At first, he wasn't going to come to the wedding, he didn't want to be witness huge mistake in marrying this awful man. But he wanted to see Justice in her wedding dress in person and not just on the front of the society page. Justice was a beautiful sight, and as she walked down the aisle, he envisioned it was he who was standing at the opposite end waiting for her and not Taryll.

Chapter 7
The Reception

While everyone proceeded to the banquet hall in the hotel, Justice and Taryll rode the elevator up to their suites to change for the reception. Justice knew she didn't want to dance the whole night in her dress; she wanted to get out of it as soon as possible, she was going to have it preserved. She changed into a cream-colored strapless gown that barely touched the floor but brushed it when she put on her heels. She loved the dress. It was the first dress she bought after Taryll had asked her to marry him. Their plan was to go to the courthouse and do a quickie wedding with the justice of the peace, but their mothers wouldn't hear of it. That was the reason it took them four years to get married in the first place. But Justice was happy with the wedding, it was beautiful, elegant, perfect. As Justice stepped into her dress there was a knock at her door.

"Just a minute, who is it?" She asked trying to pull the zipper up in the back of her dress.

"It's me babe." Taryll said. Justice rushed over to the door and pulled him inside.

"My zipper's stuck I need you to fix it." She said in a rush as she turned around. Taryll saw where the zipper had caught the fabric of her dress and carefully pulled the fabric from the zipper. He slowly pulled the zipper up her back and allowed his fingers to caress her spine. Justice smiled as she felt his fingers and then his lips caress the side of her neck.

"You know we're expected downstairs. All our guests are waiting on us to eat." She said barely above a whisper. Taryll turned her around to face him and planted his lips on hers. This kiss was nothing like the chaste kiss at the altar; it was a kiss that screamed he was starving for her taste. Justice kissed him back with just as much if not more desire to be fed of him. Her hands caressed his back and, she could feel herself going weak in the knees.

"I can't...," she breathed. "If we start this, I will never leave this room. You don't know how much my body has missed you." Justice leaned into his chest, trying to catch her breath. A part of her wanted to make the guest wait, get what she wanted, hell, needed, but she knew her mother was waiting in the lobby. Taryll kissed her neck.

"Okay we better go." Taryll said and pulled away. Justice sat down on the sofa to put on her Louboutin's, then they headed out the door and to the elevators. As they got on the elevator, she rested her head on his chest and inhaled his scent. Taryll caressed her back and prayed time would fly by so they could be alone.

Taryll and Justice walked hand in hand toward the banquet hall on the main floor of the hotel. As they arrived their wedding party and mothers were waiting. Angela gave Taryll a sideways glance before asking,

"What took you two so long?"

Before he could answer Justice said, "My zipper got stuck. I was trying to get it, but it just wouldn't budge. I know Taryll was probably waiting in the hallway a while before he finally knocked. I asked him to fix it for me. I'm the reason we're late." She squeezed his hand, looked up at him, and smiled.

"Okay well you're here now, let me let the DJ know you are ready to be introduced and then you'll walk in. The wedding party will walk in after you. Once you walk in the DJ will announce you again as Mr. and Mrs. Taryll Johnson and then you will share a kiss while the wedding party heads to the head table. After that you two will join them." Leslie said as she showed them the layout on a clipboard. Justice chuckled about how planned out this was. As she looked over the clipboard she wondered if her mother had scheduled bathroom breaks or was, she going to have to hold it until the reception was over.

Once everyone was seated the catering staff brought out the main course for everyone. Everyone was enjoying their meals and conversing, and then it was time for the father daughter dance. Justice got a little misty eyed, because the DJ was supposed to say that it was time for the bride's dance with her uncle. As she stood Taryll grabbed her hand and kissed it. She smiled and walked to the center of the dance floor.

"I'm sorry the DJ messed up baby girl." Her uncle Richard whispered in her ear. She smiled and gave him a kiss on the cheek.

"It's okay, I know he and Justin are watching from heaven." She said as she laid her head on his shoulder. When the dance was over, it was time for the bride and groom's first dance. Taryll walked to the dance floor and asked to cut in. Richard handed Justice to

Taryll, and they waltzed around the dance floor. Her mother had made her, and Taryll take a dance class to learn the waltz as their first dance, and the results were beautiful.

As the music started to fade and the new song came on the wedding party joined them on the dance floor. They all danced for a couple more songs, then it was time to toss the bouquet and the garter belt.

"Okay fellas, it is time to toss the garter belt." Taryll said as his best man put a chair in the middle of the dance floor.

Justice was a little nervous. She knew she had not felt his touch in years, well in that area of her body at least, and she just didn't know how she was going to react. Taryll walked Justice to the chair and had her sit down, then dropped to one knee then the other.

He lifted the hem of her dress, and he could see the anxiety on Justice's face. He took her hand, kissed it, and told her to relax. As he ran his hand up her dress to her thigh, he felt the garter. He slid the garter belt down her leg as he let his fingers linger at that spot on her inner thigh, the spot he knew pushed her over the edge. As he traced it with the tip of his finger, he looked in Justice's eyes as to say, wait until tonight. When he got the garter belt to her ankle, he lifted her leg and took the garter belt into his teeth and slid it over her stiletto clad foot. Everyone started to holler, and Justice could feel her cheeks getting hot. Taryll flung the garter belt into the crowd of guys and Michael caught it, then quickly tossed it to another guy in the group.

"Oh, hell naw, I'm a playa for life." He said and everyone laughed. Once the laughing died down the women started to chant bouquet. Justice smiled and walked over to the stage that was set up for the DJ. She had her bouquet in hand and started to wave it in the air as the women gathered around.

"You want this?" Justice asked smiling. The women were jumping up and down and trying to get the best spot in front of the stage. Justice turned her back to the ladies and said,

"Well, if this is what you want," then tossed the bouquet over her shoulder.

She turned just in time to see Zaria catch the bouquet. Taryll went to get Michael and Justice had Zaria in tow to the middle of the dance floor. Michael was a little hesitant about getting to the dance floor as Taryll pulled him.

"If he doesn't want to dance Taryll it's fine." Zaria said in her beautiful Spanish accent as they walked over. Michael looked at Zaria and was immediately intrigued. He was in awe of her waist length hair and green eyes. Her Spanish features were a definite turn on. She was gorgeous, her beauty almost made him rethink his earlier statement about being a player for life... almost.

"No that won't be a problem sweetheart; I would be a fool to pass up dancing with such a beautiful woman." He said as he took her hand. Zaria gave him a half smile. This player, uhuh, she thought. They started to dance to the slow song that the DJ had chosen. When the song was over, Zaria walked off the dance floor leaving Michael standing there watching her leave. Leslie got up on the stage to thank everyone for coming and celebrating in the joyous occasion.

"Now if everyone will turn their attention to the cake in the corner of the room, we will be cutting the cake next." Leslie stated then handed the microphone back to the DJ.

Taryll and Justice stood by the cake and there were so many flashes from the cameras of the photographers and the cameras and phones of family members and friends, that when it was time for Justice to feed the cake to Taryll that she had missed his mouth completely and got cake on his cheek. She slowly licked the icing off his cheek and Taryll quickly kissed her mouth.

"That was the best piece of cake I've ever tasted." He said and then kissed her again as everyone ohhed and awed over the sight of them being so flirty with one another. The catering staff cut the rest of the cake and placed slices at everyone's seats as the DJ started the music back up. Justice and Taryll walked around speaking to their guests, thanking them for coming.

Everyone was laughing and having a good time, when Taryll's mother Angela announced that the bride and groom would be leaving to head to their honeymoon in Bora Bora.

Justice and Taryll waved and thanked their guests for attending as they headed out of the banquet hall. As they were leaving Justice got the feeling someone was staring at her. As she looked up, she saw a man standing in a corner with his arms crossed, glaring at her. When she turned to get Taryll's attention to point out the man, he was gone. That was weird, she thought.

Chapter 8
Forever in the Background

He waited until the reception had gotten going, and people had already eaten, before he slipped in. He didn't want people to notice him, so he didn't talk to anyone or walk around the room, he kept to himself. He did his best to stay away from the family and close friends who were seated at the tables closest to the wedding party. He didn't want to run the risk of someone recognizing who he was. If anyone would be able to recognize him, he was sure it was her mother. He made sure he didn't say anything too revealing about himself, whatever he did tell anyone was a lie of course.

"Are you a friend of the bride or the groom?" A lady with short blonde hair asked him as he stood next to the bar nursing a Corona. He thought for a minute then answered,

"I am with a small paper in Malibu. My editor wanted me to do an article on the wedding and reception." He lied.

"Oh wow. That's interesting." The woman said as she ordered a glass of merlot.

The man took his beer and walked to another corner in the back, but before he could make it, he was stopped by yet another woman, this time older. She looked to be in her early forties. She wasn't very attractive, she was wearing a dress that was too short and too tight for her, she looked as though someone had to pour her into it.

"Hi, my name is Brenda, what's yours?" She asked with a smile. He wondered if she knew she had lipstick on her teeth.

"Eric." He lied again. He went to walk away but she grabbed his arm to stop him.

"Would you like to maybe get a drink sometime?" She asked as she leaned into him. He could tell that she had had a lot to drink already and was disgusted immediately.

"You know what girl," he said, "you are just not my type. There is a really fine man I have been eyeing all night, and just haven't mustered up the courage to ask for his number." He lied again and was having fun with it. Brenda smiled and walked away. Thank goodness, he thought and headed to a tall table in the corner with his beer. There was no other woman worth his time or attention; he had learned this fact about ten years ago.

It was time for the tossing of the garter belt and the bouquet, and he could feel his stomach churn. He watched silently as Taryll kissed Justice's hand and reached up the front of her dress. He couldn't watch anymore and headed to the men's room. As he walked out of the banquet room, he damn near ran into a woman that looked vaguely familiar.

"Excuse me." He said quickly and headed down the hall to the men's room before she could respond. He waited for the last man to leave the men's room before he punched the door to one of the stalls, imagining it at Taryll's face to soothe his anger. After a couple more punches, he splashed water on his face, washed his hands, and returned to the banquet room.

Seizing Justice

He took his place at a tall table in a back corner and watched as Taryll slipped his arm around Justice's small waist. He hated to see him touch her. He preferred it when Taryll was out of town or when he stayed at his own place. The woman he had ran into a few moments ago, whom he now assumed to be Taryll's mother, announced they would be spending two weeks in Bora Bora as their honeymoon location. That didn't surprise him, he remembered Justice talking about it when they were teenagers. Her dream had always been to go to Bora Bora for her honeymoon. He cringed at the thought of her being with Taryll. He hated him for taking her away from him. He crossed his arms and frowned just as Justice and his eyes met. She looked away and he slipped out the side door. That was too close, he thought, it isn't time for her to know I am here.

Chapter 9

Bora Bora

Justice had taken so many pictures since they gotten to the island that her memory on her cell phone was full. She had talked Taryll into buying a digital camera so she could take more pictures. She loved the island. They had just gone on a sightseeing flight over Bora Bora and Tupai and were supposed to be going out for dinner and dancing later that evening.

As they walked into their bungalow, she dropped her purse, shades, and camera on the bed. She wanted to take a shower and a nap before they went out that evening. They had so much planned, and they only had a week to do it, because the second week they were on the island they didn't intend to leave their bungalow.

"Are you really going to go jet skiing with me tomorrow?" Taryll asked as Justice came out of the bathroom wrapped in a towel from her shower. Justice took the towel off and crawled in between the sheets.

"Umm, I think I might go shopping and you can go jet skiing." She said as she got comfortable and closed her eyes. Taryll grabbed his hygiene bag and headed to the bathroom. He shook his head. Since they had been here, she had been buying different things she saw. She had already purchased some quilts, woven straw baskets, black pearls, and some local artwork. They ended up having to ship most of it back to LA.

"Jus, you have done more shopping than I thought was even possible." He laughed. "But okay, you'll be missing out. I think you would really have a good time out on the water." He said. Justice thought about it as she drifted off to sleep.

Justice ended up going jet skiing and loved it. They ended up staying out on the water for two sessions instead of just the one. After jet skiing they went snorkeling and swimming with sting rays, they had a great time, but that was the first week. After they experienced those great adventures, they just couldn't pull themselves out of their bungalow. They just couldn't find the energy to pull themselves away from each other or out of bed for that matter. Bora Bora had always been her dream vacation and it was her mother's wedding gift to her and Taryll.

"Hey babe?" Taryll called from the bed. Justice was in the bathroom brushing her teeth.

"Yeah." She said as she stuck her head out of the door.

"Let's go for a swim." Justice agreed and grabbed a little black bag. So far, she had a new swimsuit for almost every day they had been on the island, and they had been on the island for over a week. Her friends and some of the artists she worked with had given her the swimsuits as gifts at her bachelorette party. Taryll watched her take the bag back into the bathroom and close the door.

"Yet another bathing suit? Really is that all you packed?" He asked jokingly as he changed into his swimming trunks. He had brought three pairs of swimming trunks, and he thought that was a bit much.

Justice came out of the bathroom, in a black bikini. Her light brown hair was pulled into a high ponytail at the top of her head. Taryll's mouth dropped.

Where all her other suits had been boy shorts and tank tops, this one was an actual bikini that left little to the imagination. It accentuated her small waist, toned legs, and flat abs. Justice walked over to him and wrapped her arms around his neck, kissing his cheek.

The swimsuit she had on was from her maid of honor. She had been the only one to go against her wishes when she described what she liked, but with the look on her husband's face, she was going to have to thank her for doing the opposite of what she'd asked.

"If the different suits are a problem I can always…" She started. Taryll kissed her mid-sentence and told her she looked great.

"Let's go." She said and headed out the door on to the balcony. Taryll followed behind her. As she leaned against the railing Taryll came and kissed her neck, and as he was trailing kisses to her shoulders, he undid the latch and pushed her into the beautiful blue water below them. When she came up, she yelled that he was going to pay. He jumped into the water splashing her in the process. Oh, I hope so, he thought. Justice swam over to him and kissed his lips.

"I love you." She stated. Taryll took the rubber band that was holding her hair out and watched as her hair fell around her shoulders. She dunked her head under the water so that her hair would lay flat.

"I love you too. But I think I am all swam out." He said with a smile.

"We just started." She said splashing him. He kissed her and then began to suck on her neck. He swam over to one of the legs of the bungalow and Justice followed him. He leaned her up against the leg of the bungalow and started to explore the rest of her body with his lips.

"Taryll." She sighed. He paid her no mind and kept on with what he was doing. He was going to make her beg for him to stop or keep going, it didn't matter which he just loved to hear her voice.

"Taryll, please. Let's go back up to the room." She said barely above a whisper between moans. Taryll stopped kissing her long enough for her to get away. She swam to the ladder to get back up to their bungalow. As she climbed the ladder, she could feel Taryll's eyes on her behind.

"Stop looking at my ass." She said as she made it to the top then walked to their room where she started to strip out of her wet bikini.

"Why it's mine." He said as he rounded the corner to find his wife standing in the middle of the bungalow with nothing on. Justice smiled as Taryll walked toward her. He reached out and pulled her to him and started to kiss her.

"I like this view even better." Justice smiled as Taryll's hands and mouth slowly began to explore every inch of her body.

Chapter 10

Back to Reality

In nine hours, Justice and Taryll would be on a plane back to Los Angeles. She figured her mother had put them on the last flight out of Bora Bora, so they could enjoy it to the fullest. Justice woke up and rolled out of bed. Taryll was still sleep as she walked out onto the balcony to watch the sunrise.

She loved the beach, she loved the smell of the water, the feeling of the sand between her toes. She loved the way she felt when she was near the water, the sense of peace and tranquility.

The beach had always been her safe haven and to be able to experience it in Bora Bora was a dream come true. She stood on the balcony watching the waves crash against the shore, waiting for the sun to come up on the horizon.

As the sun started to rise, Justice felt Taryll come up behind her. He wrapped his arms around her waist, exhale, and rested his chin atop of her head. Justice smiled and relaxed her body into his. This morning could not be any better.

"Good morning." She said. Taryll kissed the top of her head and shushed her. They silently watched the sunrise.

Later Justice continued to pack her suitcase as Taryll talked to the front desk on the phone. She frowned as she folded her last pullover and placed it in the suitcase. She wasn't ready to go back home, back to reality, but she knew she had to get back to real life.

There was so much on her to do list back at the studio and at home. She had already called Zaria, who let her know everything was fine at the studio in Malibu and urged her not to come back to work until she and Taryll settled into their new house. Justice was tempted to, but she knew she wouldn't be able to be in Los Angeles and not go to her office. She had also called Paula at the studio in Los Angeles. Paula had let her know everything was fine, and she would see her when she returned.

Taryll also spent the morning making phone calls. He had called Ryan, in New York, to see about the studio and the calendar to find out who they were working with. Then he called Rich in Atlanta and found out his new purchases had made it to the studio and were installed and working properly. He didn't bother calling the studio in Los Angeles due to it being his personal studio and no one worked out of that studio but him.

Taryll wasn't really looking forward to going home, there was so much that needed to be taken care of, not to mention he had a trip to New York scheduled for when they got back for two and a half weeks. Ryan had found a rapper in the Bronx he wanted him to meet. He swore she could be the next Queen Latifah; and Taryll wanted to see for himself.

He was enjoying his time with his wife, without the interruptions. He looked over his shoulder at Justice, watching her check her makeup in the mirror over the dresser. He smiled; he could watch her all day.

Stephanie Tennile

"Sweetheart, you all packed?" Justice asked Taryll when he hung up the phone.

"Yeah, I finished up last night while you were sleeping." Taryll went over and kissed Justice on the cheek and grabbed her already packed bags and sat them by the door.

"Are you going to be okay on the flight back to the mainland? I know coming wasn't the best for you." Taryll asked as Justice handed him her garment bag. Justice put her sunglasses on and shrugged.

"I don't know. Every flight is different, and the flight here felt as though it was nothing but turbulence. I am praying that there isn't any on the way home. I did take some Dramamine, so that should kick in once we are on the plane." Justice picked up her purse as the bellhop knocked on the door. He and Taryll loaded the bags onto the trolley, and they headed to the front desk.

As Taryll took care of the bill for the incidentals and extras they incurred, Justice stood waiting for him. As she stood in the lobby, she noticed a man watching them. If she wasn't mistaken, he looked like the man from her reception. It can't be, she thought, and took her glasses off to get a better look. Taryll called her name.

"Yeah." She said as she looked over her shoulder at him.

"Are you ready, the car's here." He asked. Justice nodded and turned back to look, but the man was gone. Odd, she thought.

Chapter 11
Seeing is Believing

She's so beautiful, he thought. He stood next to the potted plant in the lobby as Justice and Taryll checked out of the hotel. It was the end of their honeymoon, and they were headed back to Los Angeles. Great, he thought, where I can watch her better. Being in Bora Bora with them almost killed him emotionally and financially. It took almost everything he had in savings to get to Bora Bora, but it was okay he would follow her anywhere in the world and he would pay anything to do it.

The first week was fine, they went out almost every day and every night; snorkeling, jet skiing, and dancing at the different nightclubs on the island. They had also gone to an art gallery where Justice bought a beautiful painting of a woman standing on the beach at sunset. But when the first week came to an end, they went back to their cabana, and they never came out until one day they went for a short swim and then this afternoon to leave. He could only imagine what they did to occupy their time. If she only knew how much this week hurt me, he thought as he watched her converse with one of the ladies that worked at the hotel.

Justice pushed her hair out of her face as she talked. He pulled his baseball cap down low over his shades to shield his face as he watched her. She looked amazing. Her long brown hair was straight when she had arrived, but now it was in its natural curly state around her shoulders as she wore a pair of white capris and a light pink tank top. He loved her hair when she wore it curly, it was how he remembered meeting her.

In school she rarely wore her hair straightened. She hadn't started that until about three years ago. She smiled at the lady and watched her walk away and that was when she noticed him watching her.

She saw him. He watched her as she starred at him trying to figure out if she had seen him before and if she did who he was. He saw that she recognized him and that made him happy.

He had been watching her for the past four years, but the wedding was the first time he ever gotten close to her. The first time had been an accident, but now he knew it was fate. From that point on he was obsessed with her. He followed her on Facebook, Twitter, Instagram and watched her every move. He clipped every article about her out of magazines and papers.

He watched as Justice lifted her glasses and stare at him; then she turned. As soon as she turned her back to him, he walked out of the hotel and got into a waiting taxicab, he had a plane to catch back to Los Angeles.

Chapter 12
The New House

Justice and Taryll had been in their new house in Los Angeles for a little over three weeks and still had boxes everywhere, and not to mention all their wedding gifts were still sitting around the house just waiting to be unwrapped. When they got back to Los Angeles, they signed the papers for their new house, and started to pack up Justice's condo. They decided to keep Taryll's beach house in Malibu, since Justice still had her studio there. It had taken them about a week to get Justice's condo packed up and moved and then another few days to get it cleaned up and ready to show. Justice had been dealing with her realtor since before the wedding, trying to sell her condo.

  Justice had been making calls and taking calls all day. Out of all the rooms in their new home it and their bedroom were the only rooms in the house that were unpacked and functional. Justice and Taryll had been crossing paths since they got home, and they hadn't had any time to get the other rooms unpacked. The house phone rang, and the caller id said it was her mother calling.

  "Hey Mom." Justice said into the receiver as she looked over a file about a new artist that wanted her as his choreographer. She had been reading through offers since she got back and working with a few of her regulars on videos and choreography.

"Justice, you haven't had me over to the new house yet. I can only wonder why?" Leslie said as she sat behind the desk in her home office. She was a senior partner for one of the most prestigious law firms in Los Angeles as well as a consultant for a law firm in Atlanta. Justice chuckled. Her mother was right she hadn't been to the new house since they signed the papers. Justice looked through the French doors of her home office and saw the multitude of boxes and gifts that cluttered her living room. Her sofas were still covered with the moving blankets the movers wrapped them in.

She knew her mother would be shocked to know she only had two rooms unpacked; and one wasn't the kitchen. Her mother wasn't a takeout fan, in fact she despised it.

"I know Mom, it's just everything is still in boxes." Wait for it, she thought. Justice sat at her desk and leaned back in the chair. She knew her mother would go off on her.

"You've been in the house since you got back from your honeymoon, and that's been about a month, what are you doing?" Leslie asked. She took her glasses off, sat them on her desk, got up, and went to the kitchen. She poured herself a glass of sweet tea and leaned against the counter.

"Are you back at work already?" Why ask a question I already know the answer to, Leslie thought?

"Mom, I have been back to work since the week after we got back, Taryll is in New York, and he has been gone for the last two and a half weeks. He'll be back this evening. Speaking of which, I need to check my email to see what time his flight actually lands. I want to make sure I have the kitchen unpacked so I can cook him a great dinner." Justice said, then realized she had just put her foot in her mouth.

Too late now she thought, as she pulled up her email to look for his itinerary. Her mother was going to let her have it. His flight was due to land at 7:15pm. That meant, with the congestion of LAX and the Los Angeles traffic, he would probably be home about nine.

"Justice your kitchen isn't unpacked yet? What have you all been doing since you got back?" What has she been doing, Leslie thought, this means she hasn't been cooking.

"Well, when we got back, we were invited to his assistant Bryce's house for dinner with him and his wife. Then Jerry, my studio manager here in LA, and his wife invited us over for dinner. That was the first week we got back. Then that weekend Taryll flew to New York City and has been there ever since. I have been eating out mostly because my schedule is all over the place." Justice got up from her desk and walked to the kitchen. There were boxes everywhere and she didn't even know where to begin.

"Justice eating out is not good for you. You have to do better sweetheart. Takeout food can cause you to gain weight and mess with your complexion. Have you been drinking water?"

Leslie shutdown her computer, and looked at her watch, it was 8am. Waiting for her hard-headed daughter to answer her question, she got up from her desk and headed to her bedroom to get dress.

"Mom, I eat at two places, and they are both great natural foods restaurants, plus I work out every day with my trainer, so I am doing fine." Justice opened a box. It was her dishware, she started pulling them out of the box and put them on the counter.

"Well, I am going to call your mother-in-law and see what she's doing. If she isn't busy, you will see us both in about an hour to help you unpack. There is no reason your husband should come home to a house full of boxes." Leslie finished her sweet tea and picked up her cell phone and dialed Angela.

Justice sighed; she knew there was no talking her mother out of coming to the house to help her unpack, so she said she would see them when they arrived, knowing Angela would want to come and see the house and help too no matter what she had going on.

Justice hung up the phone and placed in back on the charger. As she emptied the box with her dishware, her cell phone rang, she looked at the caller ID but it read private. At first, she wasn't going to answer the call, but she figured it could be a client of hers.

"Hello? This is Justice Rashé-Johnson." She answered. As she waited for the caller to identify themselves.

"Hello? Is anyone there?" She asked, but there was no answer then the line went dead. Justice looked at her phone and wondered if it were a wrong number or if someone was messing with her. She looked at her phone again and got an uneasy feeling.

Chapter 13
Boxes, Boxes, and More Boxes

Leslie, Justice's mother; and Angela, Taryll's mother, showed up at about 10am and went straight to work. Justice and her mother-in-law were working on the living room while her mother was decorating the guest bathroom. Justice was hanging the pictures Taryll had bought in New York a few years back, when her mother called her name. Justice put the hammer on the table and walked back to the guestroom. Justice saw her mother had already made the bed, arranged the woven baskets she had bought in Bora Bora, and taken the lamps out of the boxes and set them on the nightstands.

"Yes Ma'am." Leslie came out of the bathroom with a satisfied look on her face. She loved how she had organized and set up the guest bathroom.

"I wanted you to see the bathroom, before I crossed it off of the list." Leslie smiled.

Justice walked into the bathroom and was in awe. She knew she wanted the guest bathroom to be white with a clean feel. She bought everything for the guest bathroom in white and chrome, but the way her mother put it together was gorgeous. Her mother had the shower curtain pulled and tied back to the side of the tub and the white throw rugs were beautiful.

"I love it." Justice ran her hand along the white towels that were hanging on the towel rack near the tub. "You did an awesome job. I think it is safe to go ahead and cross it off the list." Justice smiled and gave her mother a kiss on the cheek.

"Well let me put the finishing touches on the guestroom itself and then this area will be done." Leslie grabbed another box with décor for the guestroom and started to unpack it. Justice left her mother to finish the room as she went to the kitchen to get a bottle of water.

"Justice, can you hand me a bottle of water too please." Angela called from the living room. Justice grabbed another bottle of water from the fridge and took it to Angela. The house was almost completely unpacked, and it was barely a little after three.

As the ladies finished up their individual tasks, Justice prepared her shopping list of the things she would need for her surprise dinner. As she gathered her wallet, sunglasses, and keys; her mother gathered up the wedding gifts stacking them neatly in the family room. Justice thanked them both for their help, knowing she would not have been able to finish unpacking without them. She offered to take them to get frozen yogurt, before she headed to the grocery store, but they both declined, promising to get together another day. They encouraged her to get her shopping done so her dinner would be ready by the time Taryll got home from the airport.

Justice walked them out to the car, and watched them drive off, then got in her car and headed to the grocery store. She needed to fill the fridge as well as plan her special welcome home dinner for Taryll. If she had enough time she might head to Victoria's Secret.

He watched her get in her car and pull out the driveway. He made sure she turned the corner at the end of the block before he got out of his own car and walked up to the house. Justice hadn't changed the locks when she bought the house, and he was glad. He had pretended to be interested in the realtor, Veronica, and the house, so he could get his hands on the keys to make a copy. He had been in her house a few times since she'd purchased it and since she had been back from her honeymoon.

He remembered the last time he was here; she didn't even know. He laughed to himself as he walked through the living room. Everything was unpacked and put away. He liked the way she had decorated the house. He walked into her bedroom and then into her walk-in closet, running his hands over her clothes.

The last time he let himself in was the night after Taryll had left for New York. Justice had gotten home late from the studio. He had waited down the block in his car for all the lights to go out, and then about an hour after that he let himself in. He had sat in her room and watched her sleep for a while before he had left. He closed the closet door back and walked over to her dresser. He went through her underwear drawer and grabbed a pair of black lace boy shorts, he put them in his pocket then walked out the room. He would be back; he would always come back.

Chapter 14
Welcome Home

Justice had just finished making her lentil soup and was waiting on her lamb to finish roasting in the oven when her cell phone rang. She looked at the caller ID it was a private number.

"Hello?" She answered. Justice stirred her soup.

"Hey J, it's me." Taryll said on the other end. He had just gotten off a plane at LAX and was tired. Prior to his flight he had been in the studio working with Ryan. The rapper Ryan found was as good as he stated, and he was excited about getting her started on her debut EP. Taryll wanted to have at least one song finished and a second nearly done before he left New York. He planned to "leak" the beginning of the song on the labels Instagram page by the end of the week.

"Hey Hun. Where are you?" She asked as she looked at the clock. It was quarter after eight.

"I am at the airport. My cell phone died, and I left my powerpack at the office in New York, so I am calling from a payphone. But I was calling to tell you I'm on my way home. I just got my checked bag, and I'm headed to the front of the airport. I should see, Alec, the driver that I called. Was there anything you needed me to pick up on the way?" Justice smiled, even though she could hear the fatigue in his voice, he was still thinking about her and her needs. She knew he had been working most of the day and then caught a flight home.

"No, babe, I'm fine. Just head home, so you can get some rest and unwind." Justice smiled. She walked into the dining room and looked at the table, it was perfect.

"Alright, I will see you in about forty-five minutes." Taryll hung up the phone grabbed his suitcase and garment bag and headed to the front of the airport. He saw a man holding a sign with his name on it and went to him.

"Mr. Johnson, my name is Alec I will be your driver this evening. If you'd like, I can take your bags. I am driving the black town car right over there." Taryll handed the man his bags and followed him to the car. As Alec opened the rear passenger door for him, Taryll climbed in and made himself comfortable. He would have to thank Justice for suggesting the idea of a car service to take him to and from the airport; it was very convenient, especially on a night like tonight when he could barely keep his eyes open.

Taryll felt the car shift as Alec got in the driver seat. Taryll confirmed the address and got comfortable and almost instantly was asleep.

Justice took the lamb out of the oven and let it rest as she checked her couscous; it was done. She turned the heat off under her curry and sat it to the side so she could pour it over her lamb. As she waited, she sat at the table set for two and grabbed the candles she bought earlier. They were silver just like her silk camisole and pants. As she placed them in the candleholder, she looked at the clock on the stove and noticed it was five after nine; Taryll would be walking in the door any minute. As she struck the match to light the candles the front door opened and in walked her husband.

Taryll walked in the door and sat his bags down. He looked around and noticed there wasn't a single box anywhere that needed to be unpacked. Thanks Moms, he thought. He knew Justice was just as busy as he was so the only way all those boxes were going to get unpacked was through the help of their mothers. As he walked through the living room, he saw the black and white photos he bought in New York were hanging up and he was pleased with the way the photographs complimented the furniture and accessories Justice had bought. Justice met him in the living room and reached up placing her arms around his neck.

"Welcome home." She kissed him on the lips and looked into his eyes. He looked so tired and wore out. As she held him in her arms, she rubbed his back.

"Thank you. I am glad to be home. What smells so good? It smells like Indian food; did you order out?" Taryll asked as he lifted her off her feet, carrying her to the dining room. Justice wrapped her legs around his waist, breathing in his cologne.

"No, I cooked. I thought about the Indian restaurant in Malibu we always went to and decided to recreate our favorite dishes. I made curried lamb, lentil soup, steamed veggies, and couscous." Taryll placed her back on her feet.

"Wow. I am starving." Justice took his coat off and walked to the office and hung it in the closet. When she came back, Taryll had opened the bottle of *John Duval Entity Shiraz*, the bottle was from Australia, one of his artists gave it to him as a thank you for making an almost impossible deadline for an album release.

"I thought you were saving that bottle. Wasn't it a gift?" Taryll was sitting at the table with the bottle of wine in one hand and the corkscrew in the other. Justice sat at the table and scooped some couscous onto Taryll's plate and then put a little on hers.

"Well, I think this is a great time as any to open it. We are in our first house together as husband and wife, enjoying our first home cooked meal. Plus, it compliments your lamb." He said as he popped the cork and filled their glasses. Justice placed some curried lamb and veggies on their plates and ladled some lentil soup into their bowls.

She was so excited to have her husband home. She hadn't seen him in two and a half weeks, and she really missed him. She had to figure out what she was going to do when he was gone the next time. She wasn't much of a flyer, but she may have to suck it up and go with Taryll the next time he headed to NYC or Atlanta. She had thought about opening a dance studio in NYC; she knew some really good dancers in New York, and she knew they would jump at the opportunity to be a part of her project. Justice lifted her glass and took a sip of her wine, it was perfect.

"What are you thinking about?" Taryll asked as he stared at his beautiful wife. She had her concentrating face on. She was staring out into space with her wine glass in midair.

Justice snapped out of her train of thought the second time Taryll asked his question. She put her glass back down on the table and smiled. She explained to him her idea about opening a dance studio in New York City, and how she could use it as a dance school as well. Taryll agreed it would be a great idea and suggested they look at properties for the studio at the beginning of the year.

Stephanie Tennile

"I suggest if we are both going to be traveling back and forth to New York maybe we should purchase a loft or condo in the city. You know it would save us money on hotel stays." Taryll said as he cleared the table. He really liked New York.

Justice thought about it as she got up from the table and walked into the kitchen to help put the food away. She wasn't too keen on the idea because she was a Californian at heart. The last thing she wanted to think about was possibly living in New York. If they bought a loft or condo, then Taryll would want to stay in New York more often than California.

Taryll turned around and Justice was staring off into space again. He knew she was thinking about what he had just said about the loft. He knew she loved California, but it would save them money on hotel stays. He spent a lot of time in New York due to the studio they bought, and if she was going to open a studio in New York, she would need to be there the majority of her first year once it opened.

"Justice." He said as he loaded the dishwasher.

"Yeah, I am listening. I don't really like the idea of buying a condo or loft in New York. One, it is expensive because we would be buying in the city, and secondly, I don't think we will be there often enough to where buying a loft will be beneficial. We could rent, you know, on a month to month or even a six-month lease." Justice poured the lentil soup into a Pyrex bowl, placed a lid on it, and set it to the side. She would have to wait for it to cool before she could put it in the refrigerator.

"That's true, we should rent. We aren't living in New York, and we just bought this house. Another mortgage wouldn't be a smart move right now, we are still trying to sale your condo." Taryll kissed Justice on the forehead and headed out the kitchen and toward the office.

"Sir don't get on that computer. You just got home; you need to relax. Go take a shower." Justice yelled as she poured another glass of wine. Taryll stopped midway to the office, threw his head back and chuckled. Justice knew him so well. He quietly took his shoes off and crept back into the kitchen, sneaking up behind Justice and wrapping his arms around her waist. Justice jumped, startled by his return, she didn't even hear him come back in the kitchen.

"You think you know me so well." He ran his hand under her camisole, caressing her stomach. She turned around and faced him, kissing him on his jawbone and smiled. She loved her husband and the attention he gave her. He was so thoughtful and extremely playful.

"Well, that is one thing we have in common. No matter what time it is when we get home before we go to bed, we get on that computer to check emails, send emails, delete emails." She said matter-of-factly and started to laugh. Taryll loved the sound of her laugh. He smiled and kissed her check. He lifted her up and sat her on the counter, kissing her neck and cheek.

"Well Mrs. Johnson, what did you suggest I do in place of getting on my computer? Is there something or someone else I can get into?" He asked in a low throaty voice, his eyes filled with desire. Justice smiled and kissed his lips. She hopped off the counter and walked toward their room. Taryll followed her, watching her every move.

"Well Mr. Johnson, I suggested you take a shower, relax, and unwind. You are off tomorrow and believe it or not your wife is off tomorrow as well." Justice said as she walked into their bedroom then into their master bathroom.

She turned the water on in the shower and watched as the water fell from the waterfall showerhead. She loved their shower. It was one of the many features that sold her on the house. As she checked the temperature of the water as it fell, she adjusted it to make it hotter. She grabbed a towel from the rack, dried her hands and walked over to Taryll who was standing in the doorway of the bathroom. He watched her move around the bathroom preparing the shower for him. She was so graceful. She went to the linen closet and grabbed a big, soft, grey bath sheet and sat it on the bench near the shower.

Justice walked over to her husband, watching him, drinking in his lovely frame with her eyes. She slowly undid his belt buckle and smiled as she pulled his belt from his pants and then undid the button and the zipper. As his pants hung slightly off his hips, Justice untucked his shirt and pulled it over his head. She ran her hand over his rock-hard abs, smiled then kissed him lightly on his chest.

"I love your abs." She said as she kissed his chest. Taryll went to wrap his arms around Justice when she ducked under his arm and walked out of the bathroom.

"Take a shower sir." She said with a smile. She went to close the door, but Taryll grabbed the door.

"Only if you join me." He said barely above a whisper. Taryll took her by the hand, pulling her back into the bathroom. He slid her camisole over her head and leaned down and kissed her shoulder and her neck. Justice leaned her head slightly allowing him better access and brought her hands to his curly hair. As she tugged at his hair, his kisses intensified. Taryll lifted her off her feet and she wrapped her legs around his waist. Taryll closed the bathroom door with his foot and pinned her against the closed door. He held her up with one hand and dropped his pants and boxer briefs with the other.

Kissing her again, he let her down, undressed her and led her to the shower.

Justice pulled the rubber band that was holding her curly hair up and out of her face as she walked into the shower stall. Taryll reached out and pulled her under the shower head where they were both drenched in the hot water. Justice turned her face up toward the down pour of the showerhead and paused. This feels so good, she thought but was quickly, yet pleasantly interrupted by Taryll's lips on her collarbone. Justice ran her hands up Taryll's back and then into his wet hair.

"I missed you so much J." Taryll whispered in her ear, as he grabbed her loofah and body wash. Justice kissed his chest and smiled. She had missed him too. Taryll poured her coconut scented body wash on her loofah and started to wash her back, neck, and behind. Justice relaxed under the touch of the loofah on her skin. As Taryll ran the loofah down her arm, he turned her around and continued to wash her body.

Justice took his body wash off the shelf and poured a little in her hands and worked it into lather, the smell of the citrus and woodsy undertones filled the shower stall. Taryll took her hands in his and she paused.

"What are you going to do?" He asked as he looked into the devious eyes of his wife. Justice slowly took her hands out of his and placed then on his chest and started to work the lather onto his skin in small circles. She slowly moved down to his abs and when her hands didn't seem to be stopping Taryll grabbed her hands and pulled her to him, kissing her full on the lips. He knew what she was going to do and if she did, he wouldn't want her to stop. He kissed her neck and pulled her earlobe into his mouth. As he kissed her his hands travelled down her back and cupped her behind.

"You want to play?" He whispered on her lips. "Let's play." Taryll playfully slapped her butt, and then captured her mouth with his. He lifted her off her feet and pressed her back against the shower wall, thrusting into her. He had missed her. Everything about her, but this he missed most of all, the way she felt. The way her inner muscles would clench him tight and push him over the edge.

Justice cried his name repeatedly, begging him not stop; and he gave her everything she wanted. Just as she reached her peak, so did he and they came together. He set her back on her feet, kissing her softly.

"I missed you." He said softly.

"You can't be gone that long again." She said as she caressed his cheek.

They rinsed the soap away and got out of the shower. Taryll slapped her butt playfully and she jumped a little. Taryll wrapped Justice in a towel and another around his waist. He walked out into their bedroom, and he noticed the patio doors leading to the backyard were open.

Taryll paused; he didn't remember the doors being open when they had gotten into the shower. He turned around and looked toward the bathroom with a concerned look; and Justice knew something wasn't right. Taryll walked into the room and looked around; no one was there.

"What is it?" She asked from the doorway of the bathroom. The air coming from the open doors caused her body to shiver. She looked at her husband as he walked toward the open doors.

"Did you open the patio doors?" He asked. Taryll looked out. No one was outside, but he would have to go out and look just to be sure.

"No." Justice got a nervous feeling like she was being watched. She pulled the towel tighter around her body. Taryll went into his closet and grabbed a pair of jeans and slide them on and then a tee shirt. As he stepped into his Tims he said,

"Justice I am going to walk around the yard, see if anyone's out there. Close the door behind me and call the police." Justice closed the doors and went to her closet, grabbed a sundress, and threw it on. She came back into the room and looked for the bedside phone, it wasn't on its base. She looked for her cell phone, and realized it was plugged up on the charger in the office. She opened the door of their bedroom and looked out into the hallway, no one was there.

Chapter 15
Unwelcomed Guest

Justice hurried down the hall toward the living room and to their office and opened the door, locking it behind her. She was nervous, who would break into their home, why? As she sat at her desk, to grab her phone, she got the feeling someone was watching her. When she looked up, she saw a man standing in her living room starring at her through the French doors of her office. Justice couldn't breathe, couldn't speak, she couldn't move. All she knew was a strange man was standing in her living room, but she couldn't see his face. She turned to grab the phone and started to dial, she looked up and the man was gone. Justice held the phone to her ear waiting for someone to answer.

"911 what is your emergency?" The dispatcher said once she came on the line.

"My name is Justice Rashé-Johnson, and someone's broken into my house." She said just barely above a whisper. Justice couldn't take her eyes off the living room. She could have sworn someone was standing there.

"Ma'am is the person still in the house?" The lady asked calmly.

"I, uh, I don't know." Justice said as she got up and inched toward the door. Where is Taryll, she thought as she started to pace. She hated this. When she came to the office, she didn't turn on a single light, and now she was scared to turn them on. She didn't know what she would see in her living room if she did. All the lights in the house were off except for the one in her bedroom.

"Ma'am we are sending someone out right now, please stay on the line." Justice said okay and sat down at her desk. She wanted to get up and go find her husband, but she knew she didn't have anything to use to protect herself with if she were to leave, plus she didn't know if the man was still out there. Justice wasn't short, standing five foot seven without shoes, but the man she saw was well over six feet tall. Of all the things I could have put on, a dress, she thought, as she looked down at what she was wearing. Even if she had to fight, she would be at a disadvantage.

"Ma'am are you still there?" The dispatcher asked.

"Yes, I'm here." Justice stood and walked over to the doors that separated her office from the living room. She looked hard into the darkness of her living room and did not see anything. She could make out the sofa and the coffee table, she thought she saw someone standing by the front door, but it could be her mind playing tricks on her.

"There is an officer outside your home, he's informed me he's speaking to your husband. You can hang up now."

"Thank you." Justice hung up the phone, turned on her office light. There was no one standing in the living room. The figure she saw by the door was the coat rack. She unlocked the door to her office and headed to the front door. When she opened the door Taryll came up to her.

"Did you find anyone?" She asked. Justice walked into his arms and rested her head on his chest.

"No sweetheart we didn't." Taryll said as he held her to his chest.

"Did you check the house?" Justice asked as she started to shiver. It was mixture of the cool morning air and the knowledge that there was someone in her house. Taryll looked at his wife and he knew she was keeping something from him.

"What did you see?" He asked as he looked into her eyes. Justice tried to look at the ground, but he lifted her chin with his finger.

"Justice, tell me." Justice looked at him and then looked toward the police officer standing behind her husband.

"I think I saw a man standing in our living room when I was locked in the office."

"What? Why were you in the office? What did you see?" He said with anger Justice hadn't seen in years. Justice winced at the thought of him being angry. She looked at the police officer who was standing behind Taryll again. He was talking on his radio to another officer who was walking the property.

"I needed to get to the phone to call the police. The phone wasn't on its base in the bedroom. It was dark; it could have been my mind playing tricks on me. I was scared." She said as she looked at her husband. Taryll told the officer he would appreciate it if he and his partner would do a walkthrough of the house before they left. The officer nodded and called for his partner on his radio. When his partner came around to the front of the house, they both walked in and checked every room. They didn't find anyone.

Justice sat on the loveseat as Taryll walked the officers to the door, then set the alarm. Justice was shaking again, and this time she couldn't control it. She put her head in her hands and let out a breath. She wanted to believe she had just imagined a man standing in her living room, but she couldn't shake the feeling she was being watched. First at her wedding, then at the hotel on her honeymoon, now this; she was starting to wonder if the phone calls she got yesterday were tied into this as well.

He had been in her closet when Justice and Taryll came into the bedroom. He had left the patio doors unlocked when he came earlier so he would be able to get back in. Once they entered the bathroom, he opened the patio door and snuck out into the backyard. He wanted to disrupt their evening and he wanted her to know he was watching that he was there. And now she knows, he thought as he slipped out the back door. He had stayed in the shadows, until the police officer headed back around to the front of the house. He crept down the hill and jogged the three blocks to where his car was parked.

As he slid behind the wheel of his late model Honda Civic, he reached into his pocket and pulled out a pair of Justice's lace boy shorts. At first, he wasn't going to take anything else, he had grabbed a pair earlier, but these were on the floor next to her hamper in her closet. He brought them to his nose and inhaled her feminine scent. He missed her. It had been a long time since he smelled her lovely scent.

He needed to be closer to her, he needed her to be with him. Patience, he thought, patience.

Chapter 16
Breakfast for two

Justice woke up the next morning to find Taryll was already up. They hadn't gotten to bed until almost four that morning and it was nine. Five hours, she thought, not long enough to sleep body go back to sleep. She pulled the blanket over her head with a groan and tried to go back to sleep, then she heard the bedroom door open. So much for going back to sleep, she thought.

"You're up." Taryll said as he sat on the edge of the bed. Justice curled up into a ball under the duvet and winced. She didn't want to get up, she didn't want to get out of bed, in fact she wanted him to come back to bed.

"No, you're imagining things. I'm sleep; I'm talking in my sleep. A matter of fact you're supposed to be sleep right next to me." She said from under the covers. Taryll pulled the duvet off the bed and tossed it on the floor. Justice grabbed her pillow and put it over her head. She didn't want to get out of bed her body was begging for rest, but she knew now that she was up, she wasn't going back to sleep.

"Alright Sir, you win. I'm up." Justice sat up and ran her hands through her unruly hair trying to tame it even though she knew it was a lost cause without a brush and detangler. Taryll leaned over and kissed her cheek and walked to his closet.

"You know, I would like to take my beautiful wife to breakfast if that's alright with her." He said from his closet. He grabbed a pair of jeans and a dress shirt and started to get dressed.

"Well, I'll check with her and see." She paused. "It should be fine. I am sure she has the day off." Justice chuckled as she stretched and headed to the bathroom. She relieved herself and then went through her routine of washing her face, brushing her teeth, and trying to tame her unruly curls. *It's time for me to go see Adrian*, she thought as she sprayed her hair with the detangler. As she ran her brush through her hair, her curls started to take shape. She grabbed for her hair spray and sprayed her curls and then pinned them up toward the top of her head.

When she came out of the bathroom Taryll was standing in the middle of their bedroom, fully dressed, and he had made the bed. Justice could tell he was ready to get going. Once he was ready, he figured she should be ready as well. Well, that was something he was going to have to learn now that they were married, she wasn't going to be as quick in that department as he was.

"I will be out in a minute I just have to get dressed and do my makeup." Justice said as she walked into her closet. Taryll followed her and reached for her vintage black shirt dress with the red belt. Justice went to grab a yellow sundress that she had been waiting to wear.

"Wear this." He said with a smile. Justice looked at the dress and looked at her husband. The dress still had the tag on it. Taryll had bought it the last time he was in New York.

"Why?" She asked as she took the dress and grabbed her red flats off the shelf.

"It still has the price tag on it from when I bought it for you months ago. I really want to see you in it." Taryll smiled and kissed her lightly on the lips and walked out of the closet and out of their room to leave

Stephanie Tennile
Justice to do whatever it was that took her almost two and a half cups of coffee to do.

Justice looked at herself in the full-length mirror that stood in the corner of their bedroom. She had to admit Taryll had done a great job when he chose the dress. She loved the way that it fit and accentuated her small waist. She sat on the edge of the bed and put on her flats. All she had to do was her makeup and she would be ready to go.

Taryll opened the door to the restaurant, allowing Justice to walk in before him. He was happy they had the day off; he was going to enjoy this time with Justice because come the next morning he would be in the studio at nine until lunch then he had a business lunch with a new artist at Sony Records that want him to produce a couple of tracks for his next album. After that a conference call with a new record label in Atlanta that wanted him to invest. As he thought about his workload, he started to stress a bit, but he loved what he did, and he thanked God every day he was able to do it.
"Good morning, Sir, Ma'am. Two in your party?" The hostess asked as she smiled. When they walked in, she recognized the power couple right away. Justice looked at her name tag and answered,
"Yes, Melissa, it is just the two of us."
Melissa nodded and asked that they follow her to their table. Taryll stood to the side and allowed Justice to walk in front of him. When they were seated at their table Melissa handed them their menus and told them their server would be with them shortly. Justice opened her menu and looked over the breakfast selection. She didn't have much of an appetite, so she decided on something small, some fruit and avocado toast. Taryll decided on

the country omelet with whole wheat toast, then closed his menu and waited for their server.

"Tell me what you saw last night." Taryll said as he looked at Justice. Justice sat her menu at the edge of the table so their server would know they were ready to order. As she took a breath to clear her head, she looked at her husband. He had a worried look on his face and she hated it. She didn't want her husband to worry about her. It had been a long time since she'd seen that look on his face, not since her senior year of high school.

"To be honest I don't know what I saw. It was late and the house was dark. I thought I saw a man standing in our living room staring at me in the dark. But it could have just been the coat rack in the dark." She stated. The thought of someone being in their house gave her the creeps. Since she had been in the business, she had her hand full of admirers, but she never had a stalker.

However, she was well prepared. She had been taking kickboxing and Tae Kwon Do since middle school and was a 3rd degree black belt. Then after her attack in high school she started taking Krav Maga, which she currently held an orange belt in.

"J, I don't think you were imagining what you saw." Taryll started but stopped as their server came to the table to take their order. Taryll placed their orders and asked for a coffee for himself and a chai tea with cream for Justice. She smiled. Whenever she had a stressful evening the next morning, she would have a cup of tea, if it was bad, she would have a cup of tea prior to going to bed.

"What do you mean?" Justice asked. She looked around the restaurant because she was starting to get the feeling she was being watched again, and she was, by a table of teenaged girls, at the table on the other side of the restaurant and they were starring and pointing their way. She figured they knew who they were. Justice smiled and waved at the girls.

"When I was walking around the house, I saw shoe prints in the flower bed outside of the living room window." Taryll said. Their server came back with their drinks and said their food would be out momentarily. Justice thanked the server and opened a Splenda and poured it into her tea. As she took a sip of her tea she sighed. Why didn't he tell me last night, she thought, but then quickly understood why he hadn't? If he had told her she wouldn't have gotten the few hours of sleep, she did get.

She figured she should tell him about what she saw at their wedding and honeymoon. She was a little nervous as to how he would take the news.

"Tar, I need to tell you something. I don't know if they're connected but at our wedding when we were leaving to go to the airport, there was a man glaring at me, but when I turned around, he was gone. Then when we were checking out of the hotel in Bora Bora, I could have sworn I saw him again. Then the day before yesterday evening I got a phone call from a private number on my cell but there was no on there."

Taryll looked at Justice and was furious. How could she hold onto all of this, he thought? He picked up his cup of coffee and took a large gulp, to keep from saying what he was thinking, then sat it back on the table. He was just about to ask her to describe who she saw, when their server brought their meals to the table.

Justice breathed a sigh of relief because she knew Taryll was upset that she was just now telling him this. It had been almost three months since the sighting at their wedding and honeymoon. She quickly said grace and took a bite of her fruit.

"Baby, I know you're upset. But when it first happened at the wedding, I thought it was just a fan who had gotten into the reception. But when I saw, who I think was the same man, again in Bora Bora, I got nervous. I tried to get your attention to point him out, but he was gone before I could tell you. Then once we got home, there weren't any more sightings, so I figured I was just being paranoid." Justice took a bite of her avocado toast. She looked up at her husband and he took another gulp of his coffee.

He wasn't happy, and he was trying hard not to lose his temper. Taryll wanted to yell at her and ask her how in the world she could keep something like this from him. How could she be so stupid, he thought? He took yet another gulp, finishing his coffee before he spoke.

"You should have told me, long before now Justice. I would have hired security to watch the house while I was away." He said. Taryll had pretty much lost his appetite. He pushed his plate away. To think someone was watching and following his wife, pissed him off. He thought about how he'd been gone for two and a half weeks and could feel his blood pressure rising. Everything that could have happened during that two and half weeks was running through his mind, all the what ifs. He quickly thanked God she was safe.

"I was gone for two and a half weeks J. Anything could've happened. What if this guy broke in while I was gone?" Taryll picked up his cup, realizing all his coffee was gone, sat the cup back down.

"Baby, I am fine, I was fine. You didn't need to do that. We have security at the studios, the lot, and we have an alarm system on the house." She tried to say it as calmly as she could. She could feel herself start to get upset. He acts as though I can't take care of myself, she thought as she looked down at her cup of now cold chai tea. She took a deep breath and tried to think about it from his perspective. She was wrong, she should have told him about the man she saw. He was right anything could have happened.

"That you forget to set at both the studio and the house. Hell J, you never set the alarm you had at your condo. You get so distracted or sidetracked that you barely remember to lock the damn doors." He added. Justice was notorious for forgetting to set the alarms. She was always running a million miles a minute and her mind was always occupied on the next task at hand or the next item on her never ending to do list.

"Okay, point taken, but we do have an alarm system and I will do better at setting the alarm, I promise." Justice pushed her plate away as well, suddenly she wasn't as hungry as she had been when they first sat down. She placed her hand over the top of his, trying to get him to calm down. She knew if he stewed in it too long, she would have a bodyguard following her everywhere she went, and a bodyguard at the house; and she didn't want that at all.

"Baby, I don't want you thinking I cannot take care of myself. I have been taking kickboxing and Tae Kwando since I was eleven. I am a 3rd degree black belt, and I have an orange belt in Krav Maga thanks to you. I can defend myself." Justice said and she rubbed his hand.

"I just want to know you're safe and self-defense is good but not everything. If anything were to ever happen to you, I don't know what I would do." He said as two of the girls from the other table walked up to theirs.

"Excuse me, my name is April, and this is my friend Chrissy and we wanted to know are you Justice and Taryll Johnson?" April asked with a squeal.

"Yes, we are." Taryll said. Justice nodded and smiled.

"OMG..." Chrissy said looking over her shoulder and the other eight girls who were sitting at the table came over in a rush. Taryll and Justice laughed as the girls crowded around their table. This wasn't the fist time this had happened. Once their careers started to take off and they started working with bigger named celebrities, they became celebrities in their own right.

"We are a part of the dance team at Los Angeles County High School of the Arts, and we just love your work. You have worked with so many people and have been on tour with so many different artists. Justice you're awesome!" April said. The girls were all smiling and nodding their heads. They were so excited to meet their idols.

Chrissy was staring at Taryll and then said,

"Mr. Johnson. My brother is a music lover he goes to our school too, he's a freshman. He says that your beats and creative input on the songs you produce are pure genius. Plus, I think you're super-hot!"

Taryll blushed and said thank you. He and Justice signed a bunch of autographs and told the girls they were getting ready to head out. Justice told the girls she would contact the school and see if she could come and set up a dance camp with the team and they started to squeal and jump up and down. The girls all hugged her and Taryll, took pictures, and then went back to their table. Taryll took care of the bill and told the server he would pay the girls' bill as well.

As they walked out to the car, Taryll's phone rang; it was his new artist, John Riley. He was a great up and coming R&B singer. He had first heard him on a YouTube video that a friend had sent him. It was crazy that how he found talent today. When he first started in the business he was going to different clubs looking for talent and listening to demos that were sent to him, now all he had to do was go through YouTube and TikTok videos.

Taryll looked at Justice and she told him to take the call.

"Hey John, what's up?" He fished his keys out of his pocket.

"Hey T. I was wondering, since I am in LA could we put down a few tracks today. That's if you aren't busy with anyone else." John said into his Bluetooth. He was driving up the Pacific Coast Highway, PCH to the locals.

"Give me a minute John. Let me check and see what I have going on." Taryll muted the call. He looked at Justice and gave her a look that said, I know you are going to be mad. Justice smiled and knew exactly what was going on, he was being called to the studio.

"Baby, I know we were supposed to spend the day together. But John Riley is in town and wants to work on some tracks. Do you mind if I head to the studio and knock it out?" Taryll asked.

"Tell John I said hi, I am going to give Adrian a call and see if she can squeeze me in today. I really need to get my hair done. I want it to look right since I go back to work tomorrow. Go ahead and go. It may save you from having to go to New York in a few months. Get some work done. I'll get with you later this evening."

John was usually on the east coast, but Justice was right Taryll needed to take advantage of him being in town. Justice kissed his jaw as he opened the front passenger door of his Land Rover to let her in. Taryll walked around to the driver's side and got it. He told John he would meet with him and gave him the address to his personal studio. They agreed they would meet up at two, giving them both enough time to get there.

Taryll drove back to the house to drop Justice off. On the way she had spoken to Adrian, she had an available appointment in a few hours. Justice told her she would see her then. Taryll parked the car in the driveway, got out and opened Justice's door, helping her out of the truck.

"What are your plans until you have to be at Adrian's?" He asked as he kissed her cheek and opened the garage. Justice walked into the garage and grabbed her motorcycle helmet. She didn't know how many more nice days she would have left to ride before the weather changed.

"I am going to go for a ride down PCH, and then I'll head to Adrian's. I'll call you after my hair appointment. I may go to the mall, so I'll let you know. Have a great session." She walked her bike out of the garage and left it in the driveway. She kissed her husband and then went in the house to change. There was no way she was riding in a dress and flats.

He sat in his car just a few houses down the street watching Justice get out of Taryll's truck in front of their house. She looked great and her long legs were on full display in the dress she was wearing. He imagined having her legs wrapped around his waist, her arms wrapped around his neck, and her whispering I love you in his ear.

As Taryll helped her out of the truck, he wanted to yell at him to take his hands off her, that she was his and his alone, but he kept his mouth shut. Quiet, he thought, just a little while longer. In time he wouldn't be able to touch her again.

She was his, even if she didn't know it yet.

Chapter 17
Girl Time

Justice pulled into the parking lot of Adrian's hair salon, putting the top up on her BMW convertible. She grabbed her purse out of the seat next to her and got out the car. As she locked her doors, she saw a white SUV sitting at the other end of the parking lot. She thought she saw the driver holding a camera. She started to get chills and hurried into the salon.

"What's wrong with you J, you came running in here like someone was after you." Adrian said as she walked toward the front window and looked out. Justice looked at her and smirked. Adrian walked back to her station and got the shampoo and conditioner so she could wash Justice's hair.

"I just thought someone was watching me, or at least taking pictures of me." Justice sat her purse on Adrian's station and proceeded to take her hair out of the ponytail she had it in.

"Well J, I thought you'd be used to it by now. You are a celebrity in your own right. Hell, you've worked with so many artists you can be seen in almost anything they do." Adrian walked over to the shampoo bowl and Justice followed behind her, saying hello to Trina and Shealynn, the other stylists who worked in Adrian's shop. Justice sat down in the chair and leaned back. This was her favorite part of coming into the shop to get her hair done, her time at the shampoo bowl.

Adrian had been doing her hair since she was in high school, and she knew once Justice sat in that chair there were no words that could be spoken. Justice loved to relax to the sound of the water and the feeling of Adrian's fingers massaging her scalp.

Once Justice was done at the shampoo bowl, Adrian walked her back to her station where she sectioned her hair in parts and started to blow it dry. At first there were no words spoken, and this wasn't normal for Justice. She would run her whole life down to Adrian. She would tell her everything that happened since the last time she sat in her chair. The conversation should have started already, thought Adrian. She hadn't done Justice's hair since her wedding and that was almost four months ago.

"Okay J, explain. You are awfully quiet and usually the paparazzi doesn't bother you, why is today different?" Adrian asked as she finished blow drying a section of Justice's hair.

"I don't think it's the paparazzi this time Adrian." Justice said then paused as Adrian finished blow drying her hair. As she clipped her hair up so she could start to flat iron her hair she continued.

"Last night someone broke into our house." Justice said. Adrian stopped flat ironing Justice's hair and starred at her in the mirror. Adrian's face changed. She was worried. Justice was like a daughter to her and to know someone was in her home scared her. Adrian put the flat iron down and turned the chair to where Justice was now facing her.

"What? Are you all okay, did they steal anything? How did they get in?" Adrian asked.

"We're fine, and no, he didn't steal anything. I don't know why or how he broke in. All I know is that it has me more watchful of my surroundings." Justice looked at her hands and added what she was thinking. "I feel as though this isn't the first time this guy has been near me." She looked up at Adrian who was staring back at her.

"What gives you that feeling?" Adrian asked as she turned the chair back around, unclipped her hair, and continued working.

"On my wedding day there was a man at my reception glaring at me. I didn't recognize him, so I know he wasn't an invited guest, then I swear I saw him again when we were checking out of the hotel in Bora Bora."

Adrian stopped again, again turning the chair around to face her. A man was stalking her and followed her all the way to Bora Bora, she thought, this man must be crazy.

"Are you sure it was the same guy? Are you sure it just wasn't a fan?" Adrian looked Justice in the eye. She knew Justice would say no just to ensure she didn't worry, but she wasn't expecting the answer she received.

"I'm positive. He was wearing glasses and a hat, but I know it was him. But both times I didn't get a good look at him because he was always on the other side of the room or at the hotel he was on the other side of the lobby."

"This man has spent some serious money to follow you, Justice. For heaven's sake he followed you to Bora Bora, who does that? That is not a cheap flight, and if he was there the entire time you were there… that was some planning. Be careful you hear me. Maybe you need to hire a bodyguard or security or something. I take it since you don't have any of those, you haven't told Taryll, or your mother." Adrian put her hands on her hips as she talked.

She knew how protective Justice's husband was. He had been protecting her since she was little girl. Don't let her get started on Leslie, she had already lost one child, if she had known that Justice was being stalked she would have hired someone to watch over her.

"I told Taryll this morning at breakfast about the wedding and honeymoon situations. He wasn't happy I waited so long to tell him. I haven't told my mother, and I don't plan to until I have more information. I don't want her worrying about something she cannot control." Justice said.

"I don't blame him, hell I would be straight pissed if I found out almost four months after the fact and it was only because someone broke into the house. I don't agree about how you are handling this with your mother. Leslie is a lot stronger than you give her credit for. The divorce from Aaron really strength her and grew her into the woman she is today, don't underestimate her. Plus, she could probably use some of her connections within the legal system to help figure out who this could be." Adrian said as she grabbed the comb. Justice winced. Adrian was right. She was wrong for not telling her husband about the incidents, but she could not brin herself to tell her mother.

"He was really pissed because he had just got back from New York. He was gone for two and a half weeks." Justice said, moving the conversation back to how her husband responded to the issue.

"Justice Rene, this man could have done anything to you while he was gone. If he spent all that money to follow you to Bora Bora, I wouldn't be surprised if he isn't watching you here in LA. I wouldn't be surprised if he knew Taryll was gone to New York." Adrian said angrily.

Justice stared at Adrian in the mirror, she knew she was mad at her, she had called her by her first and middle name, and she had that mom look on her face. Adrian was right, and she hated the fact she was. This man could be following her everywhere she goes, and she wouldn't know it. How long has he been following me, Justice thought?

Adrian combed Justice's hair through with her fingers as she put the finishing touches on her hair, adding a light spray of coconut oil. She stepped back and looked at her work. She loved working with Justice's hair. Her hair fell past her shoulders when it was in its natural curly state, but now that it was flat ironed; it was to the middle of her back.

"You want me to pull it into a ponytail? I doubt you are going to spend your day off any other place than your studio." Adrian smirked.

"Funny, actually you can leave it down, I might stop by the office, but then I am headed to the mall." Justice said as she pulled her wallet out of her purse. She handed Adrian two hundred-dollar bills and put her wallet back in her purse, she never asked for change, always leaving Adrian with a generous tip.

"Justice… again be careful with this man. You never know what these guys want. Plus, your mother would have a heart attack if anything happened to you. I would have a heart attack if anything happened to you." Adrian pulled Justice into her arms and hugged her tight. She loved her as if she were her own.

"I'll be careful, I promise. I've been changing up the routes I use to get places and everything; plus, I am remembering to set the alarm." She chuckled. Justice said her goodbyes to Adrian and the other ladies in the shop, put on her sunglasses, and headed out to her car. She looked at her watch it was a quarter after five; she had just enough time to get to her office and then do a little shopping.

When Justice pulled into the parking lot in front of her studio, she pulled into her car in her spot and got out. As she walked up to the door Zaria was walking out.

Seizing Justice

She had been in Los Angeles for the better part of a week wrapping things up with Monica on her new music video.

"Oh no you don't! Justice today is your day off, and I am off the clock in ten minutes. I just got Monica to leave after being here since three this morning. What are you doing here?" Zaria huffed as she leaned against the door denying Justice access to the building.

Justice laughed and told her she just wanted to grab some files from her desk to take home. Zaria shook her head in the negative and told her she needed to get off the premises before she called security in her thick Spanish accent. That made Justice laugh even harder.

"Well since you're not going to let me into *my* office, how about you grab your things, and we go and get a late lunch or early dinner." Justice said as she headed back to her car.

"Now that… that I can do. I just might fill you in about what happened today, oh and if you are really lucky, I might even let you buy the first round of margaritas!" Zaria joked as she went back into the studio and to the office to grab her purse and sweater. When she came back Justice told her they would head to Chili's, and she would buy the first round of margaritas if she told her how Monica's video turned out.

Zaria finished the last of her second margarita and was laughing so hard it hurt. She couldn't believe what she was hearing, Justice decided to work with Janae. Janae was an up-and-coming artist, and if the rumors were correct, and social media wasn't lying, this girl was a handful, hell two handfuls and a basket. Social media had her described as the spoiled brat of R&B.

"What Z? What is so funny about me working with her?" Justice took a sip of her Kettle One martini and stared at her friend.

"Justice the girl is a diva and gives everyone she works with a hard time. I can't believe you fell for the 'I am your biggest fan, and it would be an honor to work with you' comment. This girl is going to give you hell. I am so glad I am working on Ginuwine's tour and not on hers." Zaria laughed as she waved the server back over to their booth.

Zaria ordered another margarita, Justice order a coffee, shook her head, and laughed. She had read up on Janae. Social media and the tabloids really spoke negatively of her, but she had read similar accounts on other artists she had worked with and after laying down the ground rules and what she wouldn't put up with, things went rather well.

"Look, Z, I don't think it will be that bad. This is her first tour; she's excited and ready to work. Besides, when I meet with her and her team, I will have the same talk with her I do with every artist we have worked with. I'll let her know what I will and will not put up with, and what will nullify her contract." Justice said.

"If you say so J. Okay enough about work," Zaria said as she wiped the tears from her cheeks. "What is going on with you? What have you and the hubby been up to?" She asked.

"Nothing really, I know you don't want to talk about work but that's all we really be up to. Since we've been back, Taryll has been to New York, and I have been working in the studio trying to get everything in order for the next few months."

The server came back and sat the drinks on the table and Justice asked for the check. She and Zaria talked and laughed for about another hour and then Justice drove her back to the studio so she could get her car. She really wanted to tell her about the man who was following her and the break in at the house, but she didn't want someone else to be worried and worked up about what had happened. Maybe it's over, Justice thought. Hoped was more like it.

Chapter 18
The Phone Call

Justice walked into her office at her studio, at a quarter after five in the morning. She was sipping on a double shot latte as she sat behind her desk. She had enjoyed her day off and now it was time to get back to work. She had to hammer out her schedule for the next three months, as well as return phone calls and listen to some tracks so she could start penning ideas for videos and dance moves for upcoming performances and concerts. She had a full day ahead of her and if she didn't start now, she would be here all night.

She was scheduled to go on tour with Janae at the beginning of the new year, and with that she would be gone for three months. As she sat and flipped through her calendar, she noticed she needed to schedule a physical prior to going on the road. She made a note on a sticky and stuck it to her computer monitor. Justice took another sip of her coffee when her office phone rang.

"Just Move Dance studio, this is Justice." She said into the receiver.

"So, you just slide out of bed without saying goodbye?" The voice said on the other end.

Justice couldn't breathe. The voice on the other end was eerie and cold. It made her skin crawl. His voice was cold like ice, no feeling or emotion could be heard.

"Who is this?" She finally asked as she found her breath. She looked at the caller ID, but it was blocked.

She knew in her heart this was the man who'd been in her house. She also believed it was the man who had followed her and Taryll to Bora Bora and was at her wedding.

"Well, if I was your husband that would bother me. I would expect you to at least lean over and kiss me before you got out of bed. But then again, I could care less about how he feels, I hate him. He took what's mine." He said and the call ended.

Justice slammed down the receiver and a chill ran down her spine. She thought back to getting up this morning and she couldn't remember if she had leaned over and kissed Taryll or not. How would this man know this? Justice got up from her desk and walked into the studio and turned on the lights, getting things in place to rehearse with Janae for her upcoming tour.

"Hey J." Jerry, her studio manager, said as he came.

"What are you doing here? I thought you and Malia were working on a video on the lot?" Justice asked as she gave him a hug.

"I came by to get some things from the back for the set. I am going to end up transferring all the props we have here to the lot. Rehearsals will go better in the larger space with is all staged." He said as he walked toward the back of the studio to the storage area. Justice started to stretch out so she would be ready to go once her client arrived.

Chapter 19
Husband for Lunch

Justice had been working with Janae for the last five hours and they had only gotten through two of the six songs she had wanted choreographed for her concert. With all of the stopping and changing of choreography and configurations of who was standing where, Justice was surprised they had gotten that far. She was really starting to lose her patience, and she was ready for a break.

Janae was a new artist. She had blown up practically overnight. She was a YouTube sensation and Sony records grabbed her up as quickly as they could. Although she was a new artist, she acted as though she had been doing this for years and Justice was the new one to the business.

Justice had never had this much headache with an artist, and she had collaborated with some seasoned veterans in the business who were known for their short tempers and their "I know what's best" attitudes.

However, she had learned early in her career how to deal with artists who wanted to come in and tell her how to run her business. Justice was a fair businesswoman, and considered what her clients wanted from her, but she was no one's fool. She had only found herself in that predicament once, and after that contract she ensure it never happened again.

Seizing Justice

Prior to working with any new artist, she scheduled a meeting with the artist and their management team to discuss what she would and would not tolerate. At that time, she would have them sign a contract that said if certain clauses were violated their partnership would be ended and the management company and artist would be liable for 30% of the full contracted amount as a breach of contract fee.

Due to Justice being a highly sought-after choreographer and producer, she hadn't had any artist or management team fight the clause in her contracts. The 30% fee was a deterrent for most artists and their management teams because sometimes the fee could end up being a high five-figure amount.

Working with Janae had been a spur of the moment happening, which was something she rarely ever did. Although Janae had called Justice personally and practically begged her to work with her, Justice still went through her usual steps in partnering with a new client. Although Justice had fallen for the rouse Janae had put on, she met with her, and her team and the contract had been signed.

Zaria had been right, the rumors were true, and Justice was pissed for not listening to her friend in the first place. If Janae continued to make changes to the choreography, configurations, and layouts of the tour they had already agreed upon and contracted for, Justice would have cause to end their contract. She didn't want to, she knew Janae's manager, and they were good friends, but she would have no choice. This would cost Janae and her team almost $39,000, for breach of contract on top whatever it would cost to replace Justice.

Janae stopped again, and Justice motioned to Tia, her personal assistant, to stop the track. Tia handed Justice a bottle of water as Justice dropped her head, took a breath, and let it out. She knew Janae was going to be a handful, her manager Rick Garcia, who happened to be a good friend of hers, warned her, after the fact of course. That was two weeks ago. Justice called Rick a week ago and told him she was on the verge of ended their contract, but he begged her to reconsider, and that he would personally talk to Janae about her attitude. He told Justice no other choreographer would work with Janae.

"I see why." Justice had told him. After twenty minutes of Rick begging and cashing in every favor he ever owed her, Justice told him she would do it, but under one condition, that she would be able to put Janae in her place if she got out of line. Rick had agreed and begged her to do so. He had told her about how he had gotten stuck with her because no one else at the agency wanted her. She barely listens to me, he had said.

"Justice this routine for the beginning of the show has to be over the top. It has to be hot, if it ain't hot I ain't doin' it." Janae said as she high fived one of her background dancers and crossed her arms over her chest. Justice tried to look past her attitude, almost trying to justify it as her being excited or even nervous about her first concert. The routine Justice had put together was hot, the fact was Janae wasn't getting the steps and when she did finally pick them up, she was always a couple of seconds behind the music. She also had a hard time lip-synching and dancing at the same time. This was hard for any new artist; however, she didn't want to hear the correction Justice was giving or the suggestions to make it easier for her.

"Okay Janae, how about we take a lunch break, it is almost noon. Let's meet back here at about one fifteen." Justice said as she wiped her face with her towel. Janae nodded and walked out of the studio with her crew. Justice sat in the folding chair and exhaled. As her crew walked out, Tia came over with some forms she needed signed. Justice looked them over, signed them and sent Tia to lunch.

"Hard morning?" Justice heard the soft baritone she loved; it was Taryll. She got up and walked into his arms.

"It really has. I mean I have dealt with some nasty attitudes, but this artist is at the top of that list. You would think by the way she complains or gives her opinion on everything she's been doing this all her life but she's eighteen and this is her debut album. I am telling you Babe, if she keeps this attitude this will be her last time working with me." Justice said and then added,

"I'm starting to reconsider going on tour with her. Three months of her mouth, I think I'll go insane. Rick had better be happy I am doing this for him. I already have just cause to breach my contract with her." Justice said so fast that she had to take a deep breath at the end of her statement. Taryll hugged her and told her he brought her lunch. Justice grabbed his free hand and lead him to her office.

Taryll sat on the sofa in Justice's office and opened the cooler. He pulled out the turkey salad, mixed greens, and cut strawberries. Justice smiled. She always ate light on rehearsal days, and this was her favorite go to meal.

"I thought you might want your favorite; your mom made the turkey salad. Also, I need to talk to you about a video for this new duo I added to my label." Taryll said as he sat the food on the coffee table in front of the sofa. He had been trying to talk to Justice about this artist for about a week, but they had both been so busy he never got the chance.

Justice walked over to the sofa and sat next to Taryll and placed her hand on his arm.

"Later." She smiled.

Stephanie Tennile

Taryll kissed her lightly on the lips. Justice kissed him back and when he went to pull away, she deepened the kiss. Taryll pulled back a little and looked at his wife and smiled. He knew that look, he knew exactly what she wanted, or needed from him. He got up from the sofa and went to lock her office door and drew the blinds that allowed her to look out into the studio. Justice untied her top, sliding it off her shoulders and onto the table. Taryll watched her as she slowly undressed; and then he started to do the same.

"I thank you for bringing me lunch but that and work can wait, right now all I really want is you. I need you to be my distraction from everything that's going on." Justice bit the corner of her bottom lip as she met him where he stood. Taryll picked her up and laid her on the sofa and started to lightly kiss her shoulders and neck. He trailed his kisses to her chest where he took one nipple into his mouth and lightly stuck as his hand travelled to the joining of her legs. He flicked her nipple with the tip of his tongue causing her to arch her back.

Justice rose off the couch as his finger traced her clitoris. She needed him; she needed to feel him inside of her. Taryll dipped one finger inside of her and then another as she slid his boxers down his legs with her foot. As he teased Justice with his fingers, she pulled him down to her lips and kissed him hard, trying to express her longing and her need for him without words. Taryll lifted her hips off the sofa and entered her slowly.

"What do you want?" He asked as he moved slowly started to thrust in and out of her body.

"I want you." She moaned. She raised her hips higher to meet his slow thrust.

"I need you Tar, I need you... faster." She breathed. Taryll moved faster and harder until Justice was calling his name.

"Shhh, quiet babe. You don't want your crew to hear you, do you?" He said with a sly smile. It was almost the end of her lunch break, and he knew her crew would be back soon. Justice didn't care at this point, right now she needed her husband in the worst way. She needed to feel him hit that spot just right that made her want to sing, she needed him to take away all her frustration, all her nervousness, all her worry with every loving stroke. As Justice got ready to climax, Taryll slowed down and Justice opened her eyes.

"Please don't tease me." She begged, running her hand down his chest.

"Look at me. I want to look into your eyes when you come." He said as he started to thrust harder and faster, feeling his own climax coming. As they reached their climax Justice let go with a soft moan and Taryll adjusted to where he was laying on the sofa, and she was laying on top of him. They laid there for a moment trying to catch their breath.

"That was a perfect lunch break, as for the food, you can leave it in the mini fridge behind my desk. I am going to be here late into the night working with Janae." Justice said as she got up and got dressed. Taryll did the same. He grabbed Justice's dance top and handed it to her as she fixed her ponytail on top of her head.

As Taryll put the food in the fridge, he watched as Justice put her shoes back on.
"I love you J." He said, kissing the top of her head.

"I love you too." Justice looked up at her husband and smiled.

"I am going to most likely be in the studio all night. So, if you want to swing by once, you're done here that would be great... we can pick up where we just left off." He said kissing her on the forehead and Justice smiled.

"That would be really nice, I might, it depends on how I feel once this rehearsal is over. I might just head home and soak in the tub."

Taryll opened the door to the office and headed toward the exit. Justice's crew was already in the studio stretching out and talking amongst themselves as they were getting ready for the rest of their rehearsal. He gave them a wave as he headed out and they smiled. He had a feeling they knew about his *lunch* with Justice.

Justice walked out of her office and her crew started whistling and clapping. Justice smiled and laughed trying to hide the fact she was completely mortified that they were very much aware of the fact she just had sex in her office.

"Okay, let's get back to work. Janae and her crew…" she started and then dropped her head.

"Oh my God, what if it were her and her crew that walked into the studio?" She said out loud and her crew started to laugh. Justice looked up and she was completely embarrassed.

"It's okay J, if I had a husband that looked like that, girl I would be gettin' it in as often as I could too." Rene said with a chuckle. Justice laughed as she walked over to her crew. Justice could feel her cheeks get hot. She couldn't believe they were discussing her sex life.

"Umm, well we know you're not all work, you do get your play time in." Chris said with a laugh as he set out the folding chairs, they needed for the song they were working on.

"Look y'all, we aren't going to talk about my sex life; we have a rehearsal we need to get through."

"You brought your sex life to work." Zaria said as she stretched. Everyone laughed and Justice shook her head. She knew she wouldn't be able to live it down. As they got situated Janae and her dancers walked into the studio.

Seizing Justice

"Alright Justice, let's pick it up where we left off, the opening song." Janae said as she took her sweatshirt off; exposing her well sculpted abs. Justice told Candace to start the music and everyone to get in place.

"Five, six, seven, eight." Justice counted off and they were back at it again.

Chapter 20
Back to the Grind

Justice walked to the mailbox, grabbed the mail, and headed to her front door. Her feet were killing her, along with her back, hips, and head. She has decided against going to Taryll's studio, because she had stayed longer than she planned to work with Janae. Taryll hadn't made it home yet, and probably wouldn't be home for another hour. It was a quarter after one and all Justice wanted to do was get in the shower and get in the bed. So much for soaking, she thought. Luckily, she hadn't scheduled anyone for the day so she would be able to sleep in. She was starting to realize she was getting older, and she wasn't able to go as hard as she used to. She used to be able to work until two or three in the morning get up at six do her three-mile run, and head back to the studio by nine to choreograph a full song for an artist and introduce it by later that evening.

    She opened the front door and dropped her bag next to the side table and sat her keys and the mail on the table. She didn't even go through it, she didn't have the energy. Justice unlaced her shoes and tossed them next to her dance bag and headed to the refrigerator for a bottle of water. Justice saw the reminder about her meeting with Taryll and his new artists that Tia scheduled for the following afternoon in her inbox as she scrolled through her phone.

Seizing Justice

Nothing pressing, she thought, she went to the office plugged in her cell, and then headed to her room to take a shower and go to bed.

Taryll parked his Land Rover next to Justice's BMW. He was exhausted, it was after two in the morning. He had been working with a new duo he had signed to his label, Black Beats Records. The duo, Too Real, was made up of brothers, DeVon and Devante James. Taryll had heard them singing in a club in Hollywood and signed them on the spot, since then, they had been in the studio working on their debut album.

Taryll walked into the house and the alarm didn't beep. Justice, he thought. She was always forgetting to set the damn alarm. He locked the door and set it. He noticed Justice's stuff by the door and realized she must have been tired if she left everything right there. He picked up the mail and leafed through it, bills, as he went to the office to check his email and to plug in his cell. He had an email from Justice's personal assistant about them meeting at the studio at 2PM to schedule time to do a music video for the group. He quickly emailed her back asking if they could reschedule their meeting due to him being on a conference call at the same time with the studio in Atlanta. As he closed his email and shut the computer down, Justice's cell phone rang. He unplugged it and answered it on the third ring.

"Hello." He demanded more than asked. It was almost three in the morning, who would be calling her cell.

"You don't deserve her." The man said and the line went dead. Taryll tried to call the number back, but the number was blocked. He leaned back in the chair and ran his hands through his curls. First thing in the morning he was calling a security company to hire a bodyguard for Justice, whether she liked it or not.

He took a deep breath, got up, and headed to bed. He would ask her if she was receiving harassing calls in the morning.

Justice woke up slightly to the scent of Taryll's body wash. He had gotten home, showered, and was now lying next to her sleeping soundly. Justice slid over and laid her head on his shoulder, draping her arm across his chest and her leg across his. It seems as though instinctually Taryll wrapped his arm around her tightly, and with that Justice drifted back to sleep.

It was eight in the morning when Justice woke up. Taryll was still asleep, so she quietly got out of the bed and changed into her workout clothes. She went to the room they converted into their home gym and got on the treadmill. As she ran on the treadmill, she listened to Too Real's *Don't Leave*, it was the song Taryll wanted her to design the video for. It was a beautiful ballad and Taryll had really out done himself with the track, she loved his use of the saxophone at the beginning. She played the song one more time before she started her cool down. Justice switched her phone from music to the dial screen and called her personal assistant, Tia.

"Good Morning Mrs. Johnson." Tia said into her Bluetooth. Justice shook her head, for as long as Tia has worked for her, she had asked her to call her Justice, but she never would, it was either Ms. Rashé or now that she was married, Mrs. Johnson.

Seizing Justice

Tia was standing in line at Starbuck's getting Justice and Taryll's coffees. Tia knew she needed to be at Justice's house within the next hour and was running behind schedule, the traffic this morning from her apartment to the part of town Justice lived in was horrible. There had been a fatal accident on the 101 that had diverted her and added 15 minutes to her commute. She had to go by the office before heading to their house which was almost a twenty-minute drive in the opposite direction. Somehow, she had forgotten to set her alarm last night.

"Morning Tia, I am running a little behind this morning. I slept in, I was so exhausted. I just finished my workout and getting ready to get in the shower, so when you get here just let yourself in. Taryll may be in the office when you get here so the alarm may not be on. But if it is you have your code, don't you?" Justice grabbed her towel and water bottle and headed back to her room. Taryll was coming out of the bathroom and smiled at her.

"Yes, I do. I am running a little late myself, there was an accident on the 101. I should be there in about an hour, an hour, and a half at most." Tia grabbed the drink carrier that held her order off the counter and told the barista thank you. Justice told her it was fine and ended her call. Tia was a great assistant. Justice removed her Bluetooth putting it on her dresser.

"Morning Sweetheart." Taryll called from his closet. He grabbed a pair of Air Force Ones and threw them on. He had a lot to do today, and he wanted to get the call into the security company while Justice was occupied.

"Morning, Babe." Justice called over her shoulder as she went into the bathroom and ran a bath. She poured a good amount of coconut oil and Epson salt into the hot water.

"You alright?" Taryll asked as he stuck his head into the bathroom. He could smell the coconut oil from their bedroom.

"Just a little sore. We had a hard rehearsal last night. We rehearsed a song where Janae is up in the harness for her to get the routine, I had to get up in the harness to show her. It has been a long time since I have done harness work and now, I remember why." Justice said as she turned on the cold water to even out the temperature. Taryll came over and kissed her forehead and told her he would be in the office if she needed him.

Justice turned the water off and took her workout clothes off, throwing them on the floor. She stepped into the tub and lowered herself into the soothing water. Oh, I am getting too old for this, she thought. She laid her head back against the bath pillow and closed her eyes. The heat from the water felt good on her body.

Justice was only twenty-seven, and she knew she wasn't old, but her body has taken a beating the last eight years. She has been dancing since she was in middle school, running her studio since she was twenty and has been going on tours with artists since she was twenty-three; what she really needed was a break from her job. Some time to just relax and allow her body to recuperate from all the work she had put it through, but when would she find the time to do that was the multi-million dollar question.

Justice rubbed lotion on her body and then put on her robe. She looked at the clock next to her bed, it was

9:30am, she sighed, she was behind schedule. She was supposed to meet with Tia at 9:30am. She wanted to get this meeting out of the way, because she had purposely kept her schedule open today. She planned to do absolutely nothing.

She knew Tia was probably waiting in the office or the living room for her, so she rushed into her closet and grabbed a pair of skinny jeans and a cream-colored sweater. Summer was officially over, and to her surprise it was feeling like Autumn. In California, it didn't really get cold... just cool. Autumn was her favorite season. Justice was excited she would get the chance to wear her sweaters and boots.

Justice grabbed her brown knee-high boots and headed to the living room. Just as she thought Tia was sitting on the sofa going through her calendar waiting for her.

"Good Morning Mrs. Johnson. I put your coffee in the microwave; it should be done in just a second. I also brought your datebook and the mail from the studio." Tia said as she got up and followed Justice to the kitchen. Tia loved her job and had been working for Justice for the past year and a half. She had been a fan of Justice's work for as long as she could remember.

When Tia applied for the job, she didn't think in a million years she would get an interview, let alone the job, but she had. She had interviewed with four other women and two men. When she sat outside of Justice's office waiting for her turn to interview, she watched as the other women focused on what they were going to say and the men were talking about how it would be to work for Justice and how sexy they thought she was, but Tia was watching the dancers in the studio.

She had always been into dance and music it was like breathing to her, so she understood the name of Justice's company. As she continued to watch, one of the dancers asked her to come over. Tia pointed to herself, and the dancer nodded. Tia sat her resume and purse in her chair and walked over to the dancers.

"Hi, I'm Zaria Morales. I noticed you were watching us rehearse, what do you think?" She asked as she wiped her face with her towel. Tia didn't recognize Zaria as Justice's right-hand choreographer and one of her best friends at the time.

"Well, I thought the steps were awesome, but the configuration of the dancers is a little off. The guys should be intermingled with the women if you are going to break into the couples at the midpoint of the song. The movements wouldn't have to be so big and jumbled when the dancers are pairing off." Tia said covering her mouth when she realized what she had said and who she said it to. She didn't mean to insult her, or her work but she did see the transitions were a little labored.

"I'm sorry, I didn't mean to criticize your work. You are an amazing choreographer Zaria." Tia said as she looked at Zaria.

"It's okay. I think you'll be a great addition to the team." Zaria said and then nodded her head.

Tia watched as Justice walked out of her office, past the other men and women waiting to be interviewed, and over to where she was standing with Zaria. Justice stuck her hand out for Tia to shake. Tia shook her hand and was awestruck. This was Justice Rashé; she was one of the best choreographers in the business, and a video producer that everyone wanted to work with.

"Thank you for coming out." Justice said, and then continued. "I have been told I need a personal assistant. At first, it was because I was trying to do too much on my own, and as the company expanded, I was being pulled into too many different directions. I won't lie at first, I didn't want to hire an assistant. I like doing things on my own, I am a perfectionist, and I can't blame anyone but myself if something isn't done or if I fail." Justice said as she looked at Tia.

Tia smiled and Justice continued.

"But I realized my family, friends, and staff were right. I was working myself too hard, and I couldn't do it all on my own. So, I started looking for a personal assistant that would be able to help keep me organized, on task, and do some of the clerical work in my office. I read your resume and I can say you will be able to do all of that. I noticed you were here fifteen minutes prior to your interview time, and I appreciate that very much. For me time is precious, I have things that need to be done and done in a timely fashion. But what drew me to you out of all the other applicants is the fact you have experience with music and dance. You have a degree from UCLA in choreography, and that is a hard program to get into. Your organization and your love for music and dance is going to be a tremendous help to me and my team."

"You also have a great eye." Zaria started. "You were able to pick up on the configuration issue I orchestrated. You know what to look for that's a plus, because there may be times when Justice will ask your advice about a project, and you'll have to be able to tell her exactly what is wrong or right with it. You can't allow yourself to be so in awe of who she is not to tell her the truth."

Tia was speechless, Zaria Morales and Justice Rashé, were complimenting her on things she didn't see in herself.

"If you are willing, I would like to try a trial period of two months. At the end of that two months if you are satisfied with working for me and I am satisfied with you working for me, we can continue on."

Tia was speechless. This had been a test. The other men and women never once gave the dancers any attention while they waited for their interview and were now very upset as security escorted them out of the building.

"I would be honored to work for you Ms. Rashé." Tia said with a smile.

Justice took a sip of her coffee as she sat at her dining room table with Tia going over her schedule. She had meetings, appointments, costume fittings for Janae's tour, and so many other things on her schedule she need to track. The table was covered with her personal day planner, studio calendar, work cell phone, personal cell phone, and tablet.

"Mrs. Johnson, your husband was scheduled to have a meeting with you about the video for Too Real at two this afternoon, but he will be on a conference call with the studio in Atlanta at the time, so he is asking if we can change the meeting time."

Tia said as she looked at the printout of Justice's hourly calendar for the day. She knew today was Justice's day off, but even on her days off they still got together to set the schedule, whether over the phone or in person. Justice loved and needed to be organized. If things weren't, she had a difficult time functioning.

"Well, we have the story boards completed for the video; all we really need to do is present. The presentation might take about an hour and half to two hours depending on any questions or ideas they may want to incorporate. Can you send him an email with three different times over the next two days he can choose from? It has to be within the next two days, because at the beginning of the week I am going to be very busy, I am scheduled to work with Janae for the next three weeks straight to get her, her crew, and the dancers ready for her concert by the end of the year."

Tia nodded and flipped through Justice's date book and chose three different times and ran them by Justice and they agreed and penciled Taryll into all three until he got back to them with a definite. Justice took another sip of her coffee and looked over the mail from the studio and gathered up all the bills.

"If you give me a minute, I'll grab the checkbook and you can mail these off." Justice was old school according to her assistant, she still wrote checks and mailed them to their recipients, while everyone else paid their bills online or by electronic draft. She got up from the table and went into the office where Taryll was on the phone with his own assistant, Bryce Collins. They seemed to be doing the same thing she and Tia were doing, but Taryll's assistant was much busier than Tia, he had to keep track of schedules for New York, Atlanta, and Los Angeles. She wondered how his assistant was able to manage it all.

Justice grabbed her company checkbook and headed back to the dining room. Tia was on the phone with Jerry. As Justice waited for Tia to finish her call, she wrote out the checks for the different bills and finished her coffee. Justice sealed the last envelope when Tia hung up the phone.

"That was Jerry, he said they just wrapped up Mya's new video and they are going to send it to editing."

"That's great they finished a day ahead of schedule. Can you please send Jerry a text and tell him that he, Malia and the crew can take the next three days off please?"

Tia sent Jerry a quick text message and then gathered up all the schedules and the bills that needed to be mailed off. Tia told Justice if she needed anything to call her, and that she would call her tomorrow. Justice walked her to the door showing her out.

Justice went back in the living room to lay on the sofa. She had a headache, and she was nauseous. Oh, I can't be getting sick, not now, she thought. As she lay on the sofa, Taryll came out of the office on his cell phone and headed to the kitchen where he warmed his coffee. Justice watched him as he conducted his calls and walk back and forth between the kitchen and their office before, she drifted off to sleep.

Taryll walked into the living room as he hung up with his personal assistant, Bryce. He still needed to talk to Justice about the call she got last night, and the fact he was meeting with the security company to interview bodyguards to keep her safe. If someone was harassing her, he needed to know, not just because he was her husband, but to also let the security company know what the threat was. But when he came in the room Justice was sleep on the sofa, and lightly snoring. She's exhausted, he thought, that's the only time she snores. He leaned over and kissed her on her cheek. He thought about carrying her back to bed but knew as soon as he lifted her off the sofa she would wake up. He went to the office and wrote her a note.

J, I went to the studio for a couple hours and then I have a conference call. Enjoy your day off.

Seizing Justice
Love, Taryll

Taryll left the note of the coffee table in the living room where she would see it when she woke up. He gathered up what he needed to work on with the duo and headed out of the house, setting the alarm as he left.

Justice woke up and noticed it was late afternoon. She sat up and stretched. She saw the note from Taryll on the table and then headed to the office, where she spent the next couple hours emailing artists and crew members back. Jerry had emailed her to inform her of the progress of the editing of the Mya video, and her assistant emailed her to let her know that Bryce, Taryll's assistant got back to her with a date. Justice looked at her calendar on her phone and inputted the date and time of the meeting with her husband and chuckled to herself. They had gotten so busy with work they couldn't even schedule their own appointments with each other. Justice was glad they had such efficient assistants but sometimes she wished they could go back to the days when they did it on their own and their days weren't so overrun with appointments, rehearsals, and tour dates.

Thinking of tour dates, she needed to assure Janae and her management she was going to do the concert at the beginning of the year. Justice sighed as she started to compose the email to Rick, Janae's manager, then she stopped. She quickly sent an email to her assistant asking her to contact Janae's manager, Rick, and see what the exact dates were, what all her company needed to provide for the tour, and what were the locations, so she could book her hotel rooms prior to. Justice sat back in her desk chair and exhaled. Right now, what she really wanted was some crispy duck and rice from the Chinese restaurant over by her studio. She wasn't a big fan of duck, as a matter of fact, she hated the taste of duck, but she was craving it. She grabbed her car keys, boots and headed to the living room to get ready to head to the restaurant.

Chapter 21
Misunderstanding

The meeting with Taryll and the group went great. DeVon and Devante loved Justice's ideas for the video and felt she had captured exactly what they wanted to portray to their fans. After the meeting Justice took the duo and her husband to dinner to celebrate their coming together on the project. She decided on the Chinese restaurant by the studio and again ordered the crispy duck with rice.

She just didn't understand the reason behind the craving. Even her husband had noticed she was eating the same dish for the second time this week.

Taryll sat in his office finishing up paying the bills for the recording studio. He had a great meeting with the private security company the day before. He met with the owner Juan Alvarez, he suggested he meet with two bodyguards he just hired: Mike Ryan and Gage Simmons. Ryan was ex- special forces for the Army, and Gage was an ex- criminal investigation command agent for the Army. They had recently retired from their military careers and were working in the private sector as personal security.

Taryll read over their resumes and was satisfied with what he saw. He was scheduled to meet with both the following morning. He had yet to tell Justice of his plan. He would rather ask her for forgiveness after he introduced her to the bodyguard he intended to hire, than ask her permission. If he had asked her about it, she would say it wasn't necessary.

Taryll was walking back to the studio when Rain walked in. She was an artist he and Craig heard at a club a few months back and decided they wanted to see if she would be a good fit for the label. He didn't have anything on the calendar for her today, but he had told her the next time she was in the area to bring her lyrics by.

"Hi Taryll." She said as she took her jacket off and laid it across the sofa.

"Hi Rain, how are you?" He asked as he gave her a hug.

Rain was a beautiful woman; by looking at her you would think she was a model. She was five foot nine, light skinned with green eyes and short light brown hair. She was a true talent and was able to sing anything Taryll had thrown at her so far.

"I am good. I brought my lyric book with me this time. I just don't have music to go with them." She sat on the sofa and watched as Taryll flipped through her notebook.

She loved the look of this man. He was sexy, smart, talented, and sweet. The biggest thing that drew her to him was his love for music. She was attracted to him more than she was willing to admit. She has always been attracted to men that were either no good for her or were unavailable, and she knew Taryll was very much married.

She wasn't used to working with just him, Craig, his partner, was usually in the studio too. She had purposely come by unannounced and unscheduled hoping to catch Taryll alone. She had gotten what she had wanted. As he flipped through her book, he stopped at a song entitled Next Time Around. As he read the lyrics he paused. He was intrigued by the lyrics.

"I have to hear you sing this one." He said as he handed her back her notebook. Rain looked at the page and smiled, *Next Time Around* was one of her favorites. As she started to sing Taryll sat back at the boards, grabbed his notebook, and started to note the different instruments he wanted to accompany her voice for the song.

"Next time around I will love you better babe." She sang the last line and then opened her eyes.

Taryll loved the song. It was hot and it would be a great ballad. The song and the ideas running through his head were really pushing him in the direction of offering he a contract. Taryll grabbed a track he had already made for one of her other songs, *Last All Night*. As he played the track, he told her the ideas he had for the song, and she loved them.

"Alright then get in the booth and we'll see what it sounds like." He said as he stopped the track. Rain got up and walked into the booth, sat on the stool by the microphone. As soon as she put the headphones over her ears, she heard Taryll's voice asking if she were ready. I could get use to that voice in my ear every day, she thought with a smile, as she nodded her head in the positive.

Justice had made sure everyone had the steps and scheduled another rehearsal for the day after tomorrow. Everyone had worked so hard for the last few days she felt they could use a day off. Not to mention, she had things at home she needed to take care of before Taryll took off to Atlanta in a couple days.

She told Janae she was going to look hot during her concert, and that seemed to make the young star happy. After Janae and her dancers left Justice had a quick meeting with her crew and then told them to head out for the night.

It was now a quarter to midnight, and Justice was sitting at her desk answering emails from different artists or their management teams. Justice looked at the stack of mail sitting on the corner of her desk and decided she might as well go through it while she was here. She wasn't planning on coming into the office or the studio the next day.

As she grabbed the envelope off the top of the stack the others fell to the floor. Justice sighed and got up from her seat and started to pick up the mail. As she gathered them together her office phone rang. She grabbed the receiver and straightened back up.

"Hello?" She said. No one would be calling this late other than Taryll.

"It isn't a good idea to be in the office all alone Justice. You never know who could be waiting for you outside."

Justice froze, someone was watching her. As she sat the mail on her desk, she looked out the window and into the studio. No one was there.

"You know Justice, I miss you. I miss the smell of your hair and the way you smile when you talk about music." The man on the other end said.

"Who are you?" Justice asked in a whisper.

"All in due time J, don't be scared. I would never hurt you; I love you." He said and then the line went dead. Justice looked at the phone as if it were alive. She placed it back in the base and started to gather her things.

Nope, I am not staying here alone, she thought. After she threw the mail in her bag and put her sweatshirt on, she called the house and got the machine.

"Well, I am not going home. Not to sit by myself." She said to herself. She took her keys out of her desk drawer and grabbing her bag as she walked out of her office. She locked the door and headed to the front of the studio. When she got to the front, she turned the lights out and opened the door. She looked around the parking lot. It was empty; the only car was her own. Justice quickly locked the door to the studio, hit the unlock button on her key ring and swiftly got into her car. She put her bag on the seat next to her and put the key in the ignition.

Justice pulled out of her parking spot and headed to Taryll's studio. She was scared. It was time for her to stop acting as though she could handle any and all things that came her way. She was going to tell Taryll about the phone calls and tell him that the man was still watching her and now she had proof.

At least I can go to sleep on his sofa if he still has work to do, she thought. She knew Taryll would probably still be working when she got there, but she didn't care, at least she would feel safe and could rest.

Taryll wiped his eyes. He could feel the fatigue hitting him. He had been in the studio with Rain all evening. They had stopped and ordered pizza, ate, and talked. Rain was down to earth. They had so much in common and she knew more about music than she let on. Taryll tapped his fingers on the table. He could tell Rain was getting tired too because she was starting to drag.

"Rain, we need to do that last chorus one more time. I need you to put some feeling in it, it's dragging right now." He said into the microphone. "You are starting to just sing the words that are written, and I know that's not the type of singer you are. We get this and you can go home."

Rain nodded and waited for him to run the track back. She was tired; they had been at it all evening. They had done an acapella version of the song and were now working on putting her vocals with the track. It was a little harder than she thought it would be. Instead of the musicians following her she had to follow the music and she had to redo some parts because she was behind the track and not with it.

She belted out the last chorus again. This time she sang it the way she would have if he were the man she had written about, the man she wanted to spend all night with, singing.

Make it last all night, baby take your time
Make me want you more and more babe
Make it last all night, make my body cry
Make me scream your name.

"That's it; that was perfect. Come out here so you can hear it." Taryll said as he started to work with the different parts of the song.

Rain put the headphones on the music stand and came out of the booth and sat on the sofa. She wanted to hear what it sounded like. She was so anxious. As Taryll ran it back so she could hear it she got up and started to pace.

"What's wrong?" He threw over his shoulder as he continued to work with the track.

"I'm a little nervous. I have never heard myself recorded before." Rain stopped and leaned against the boards where Taryll was working. She looked into his eyes and felt as though she were going to faint. She had never felt like this with a man. She has always found something to be attracted to, but feeling head over heels attracted, this was a first. Just my luck he's married, she thought.

"Don't be nervous, you sound great." And with that said he hit play and started the track so she could hear it. As Rain stood there she was in awe at the sound of her voice on the track; she loved it. Taryll looked at her and her facial expression hadn't changed from the time he started the track. As the track ended, Taryll turned in his chair to face her.

"So... what do you think?" He asked. Rain looked at him and smiled. She fell into his lap and put her arms around his neck squeezing him in the process.

"I love it, it's perfect, this night was perfect... you are perfect." She said and then leaned in and kissed him. As she leaned in and kissed him the door to the studio opened.

Taryll pushed her away from him and looked past her to the door. Justice was standing in the doorway. Rain got up from his lap and backed toward the door to the booth. She knew Taryll was married but at the time she didn't care, she wanted to see what it was like to kiss him; but the look on his wife's face made her hate herself for what she did.

Taryll stood up and went to Justice.

"J, it isn't what it looks like." He said, but by the time the words left his lips she had turned and walked away. Taryll followed behind her catching her arm, as she walked out the front door to the parking lot.

"Don't touch me, Taryll. Don't, Don't you dare!" She said as she pulled away. She wiped the tears from her eyes with the sleeve of her sweatshirt. She wasn't a crier, and the last thing she wanted was for him to see her cry, to see how much what she saw had affected her.

"Justice please if you would just let me explain." Taryll pleaded with her, but he knew she wouldn't want to hear it because he shouldn't have let it happen in the first place.

Justice walked to her car and went to get in when she turned with so much pain in her eyes, Taryll could feel himself dying inside. He reached for her again, but her eyes narrowed, and he dropped his hand.

"We have never, ever, dealt with anything like this when we were dating. You never worked with a woman by yourself in your studio when we were dating. Now that we're married, do you think you can do what you want because now you feel I am obligated to stay?"

"Obligated to stay?" He parroted. Taryll cringed at her words. He had never heard her say anything so mean.

"You aren't going to treat me the way your father treated your mother!" Justice covered her mouth; she didn't mean that. Taryll's father was a cheat prior to him leaving his mother, and Justice knew from all the stories Taryll had told her in confidence how he felt about his father. She knew Taryll was nothing like his father, and his greatest fear was ending up like him. How she wished she could take back her last statement. The disbelief in his eyes quickly changed to anger and she wished the ground would open and swallow her whole. He looked at her with so much anger she thought he was going to exploded.

"Baby I didn't mean..." she started but Taryll stopped her. She reached for him but this time he was the one to recoil.

"You of all people Justice... you... get the hell away from me. Go to hell!" He shouted as he walked back to the studio.

"Taryll wait!" She called out, but he ignored her. Justice watched him walk away and cried. The kiss she witnessed hurt but what she just did to him hurt her so much more. Justice chastised herself as she got back in her car. Gone from her mind was the phone call, the fear she felt, the safety she desired from her husband; now all she could think about was the fact she had hurt her husband more than he had her. Justice cried as she pulled out of the parking lot and headed home. How was she going to fix this?

He followed behind Justice when she left her office. He noticed she had gone right instead of left toward the highway and realized she was headed to Taryll's studio. Great, he thought, but continued to follow her. He watched as she parked her car next to Taryll's SUV and get out of the car. She threw a glance over her shoulder. She is checking to see if she is being followed, he thought, shit, I over did it. He hadn't meant to scare her, but he had and scared her right into the arms of her husband. This may be the last time I am able to get close to her, he thought. He knew from experience how protective Taryll could be and knew by this time tomorrow she would have a bodyguard, security, or something. At least, that is what he would do if the tables were turned.

As he sat and watched from his car at the other end of the parking lot, he couldn't help but smile. Even at night she was gorgeous, her long hair was in a high ponytail, and she wore leggings and her oversized sweatshirt. He was just about to leave when he saw her when he saw her storm back out of the studio. Something happened, some type of fight. This could work in his favor, he thought, because now he could accelerate his timeline.

After Justice pulled out of the parking lot, he waited a couple minutes and followed behind her. He only hoped she was headed home.

Chapter 22

Snatched

Justice woke up the next morning, the sun shining through the French doors of her bedroom, and Taryll wasn't home; it didn't even look as though he'd even been home. She went into his closet, everything was there. He's coming back at least, she thought. She sighed a sigh of relief as she headed to their home office. She sat at her computer and checked her email, nothing new. She leaned back in the chair and yawned.

She had spent most of her night crying about what she had done. She never wanted to hurt him, but she had hurt him. What she said last night was the worst thing she could ever do. She picked up her cell phone, she had no missed calls or text messages, and there were no missed calls on the house phone. He hadn't even called to say he wasn't coming home, she thought, he is pissed. Justice picked up the phone and dialed his cell. The phone rang and rang and then went to his voicemail.

"You have reached Taryll Johnson, I'm busy at the moment but if you leave your name and number, I will call you back."

"Tar, it's me. Baby I'm so sorry for what I said last night. Please call me." Justice hung up the phone, sent him a quick text, and went back to bed, she didn't have the energy to do anything else.

Stephanie Tennile

When Justice woke up the second time, she was cold. She opened her eyes, and the French doors were open. She sat up in her bed and looked around the room. Everything was in its place, nothing was missing, and there was no one there. She hurried to the door and closed it, locking it in the process. She grabbed her sweatshirt pulling it over her head. She walked through the whole house, and no one was there. She looked at the house phone and there were no missed calls. She grabbed her cell phone off her desk, Taryll hadn't called.

She called his cell phone and let it ring until it went to his voicemail, she didn't leave a message. She got ready to dial his brother Brandon but decided against it. She didn't want to explain what happened, especially if Taryll hadn't spoken to him yet.

Justice went to the bathroom, splashed water on her face and then relieved herself. She washed her hands and dialed Taryll's cell phone again. This time it went straight to voicemail.

"Baby, it is five fifteen in the evening. I am worried. I haven't heard from you, you aren't answering your phone, where are you?" Justice said to his voicemail as she walked back to her bedroom. When she walked into her room her patio door was open again. Justice paused in the middle of her room. I locked that door, she thought. As she went to back out of her room, she heard her room door close behind her.

"It is good to have you alone sweetheart." The man said. Justice froze.

Seizing Justice

"Baby help me." She said into her cell phone.

"Oh, that's no good." The man said as he moved toward her. Justice ran toward the patio door, but she didn't move quick enough; the man grabbed her from behind. Justice fell to the floor and the man pinned her, placing his knee in the small of her back. She went to scream but he covered her mouth with his hand and shook his head no. Justice tried to get from under him, but he was too heavy and then suddenly he had her in a sleeper hold. As she tried to fight her way out of it, something she was taught never to do, she felt herself fade and then there was a flash of a baby.

Chapter 23
Brotherly Advice

Taryll, still pissed with Justice for what she said, decided he would go and sleep on his brother's sofa. He knew he wouldn't be able to stay there long; he and his wife had been like newlyweds since they got back together after that had been separated for almost a year and a half. As he lay on the sofa his nephew came rushing into the room.

"Hey Uncle T. Why are you here?" Brandon Junior asked as he grabbed his backpack and a banana out of the fruit bowl.

"BJ, why are you late?" Taryll asked as he stretched his arms above his head. Brandon Junior shrugged, peeled the banana, and was headed out the door to the bus stop. His brother walked into the living room and leaned against the door frame.

"You know your nephew makes a good point, why are you sleeping on *my* sofa instead of in *your* bed at *your* house with *your* wife?" He said as he came over and sat in his recliner.

"Well, I can't talk to BJ about what happened, but I did want to talk to you about what happened." Taryll sat up and threw the blanket off and onto the sofa. He got up, folded the blanket then sat on the end of the sofa closest to Brandon's recliner. Brandon looked at his brother, waiting for him to go on.

Obviously, something had happened. Even though Brandon's place was close to Taryll's studio, it would have only taken him an additional fifteen or twenty minutes to get to his own house. Taryll hardly ever stayed at Brandon's house, even though the option was always there, it was part of the reason he had a key. Brandon looked at Taryll and knew he was upset about whatever it was that had happened the night before.

"Well, last night I was working with a new artist, Rain. I had just finished working on some tracks for her and wanted to get her in the booth. I didn't call Craig or Bryce to sit in on the session." Taryll looked at his brother and he saw the glint of understanding in his eyes.

"I see where this is going." Brandon said and threw his head back. Taryll knew what Brandon was thinking and had to hurry and fix his thought process.

"Now wait B, I didn't and don't have any feelings for this woman and I didn't do anything with her. But we ended up working late into the night and at the end of the session I played the track back for her to listen to. She loved it and she fell into my lap and kissed me. When she kissed me, Justice walked in." Taryll said and he dropped his head into his hands.

"How in the hell did you let that happen T? As long as I can remember, as long as you have been working you have never EVER worked with women in the studio without someone else being there. That's your number one rule, just to keep from having incidents like this from happening or false accusations popping up man." Brandon was pissed. There was no way Taryll was going to go through what he and his wife just went through and was coming out the other side of.

"Taryll, didn't what I went through with Sharon teach you anything?" Brandon asked as he wiped his hand down his face.

Stephanie Tennile

He and his wife Sharon had separated two long years ago because he had had an affair with, Rebecca Stanley, a woman he worked with. He and Sharon didn't believe in divorce, but she had put him out until he made up in his mind what he wanted to do. At the time his affair had started he wasn't interested in breaking things off with Rebecca, but he wish he had, because he missed a lot in the year and a half he had been away. He was selfish.

When he finally made up in his mind he wanted his family, Sharon had taken him back, that was six months ago. They were working on their marriage, going to counseling and being open and honest about everything.

"I didn't kiss her back." Taryll said trying to make what had happened less than what it was, but he knew that it wouldn't.

"I doubt it looked that way to Jessy." Brandon said using his childhood nickname for Justice.

"What did she say?" He asked as he got up to fix a pot of coffee. Taryll followed him into the kitchen. As Taryll took a cup out of the cabinet he heard his phone ring, from the ringtone he knew who it was without looking. He looked at his phone sitting on the counter.

"Who is it? Rain?" Brandon asked as he leaned against the island.

"No, it's J." Taryll leaned against the counter. He couldn't deal with his wife right now. He was still pissed with what had happened last night. She shouldn't have said what she said. Was she just waiting for him to mess up so she could throw it in his face? Taryll knew that wasn't the type of woman she was. She was hurt, and he couldn't blame her, she had every right to be, he fucked up. He could only imagine if it were the other way around.

He remembered when she worked with Trey Songz on his last tour, she did a provocative dance routine with him, and he was pissed. When he told her how he felt she took herself out of the routine and asked one of her other dancers to fill in.

"If she's calling, she is probably worried about you, why aren't you answering? Why are you avoiding her calls? Shouldn't it be the other way around?" Brandon was confused as hell; this made no sense to him at all. Why was his little brother ignoring the calls from his wife, when he was the one who fucked up? There was something he was missing, something Taryll was leaving out.

Taryll sighed and thought about last night and slammed his fist against the counter.

"Wow Tar hold up man. This is my house, don't break my countertop." Brandon said as he stepped toward his brother. He had never seen his younger brother this angry.

"Sorry, it was just what she said last night that I'm still pissed about. She told me I wasn't going to treat her like Dad treated Mom." Brandon stopped what he was doing and looked at Taryll. He knew that was his baby brother's biggest fear, ending up like their dad. Brandon put his hand on Taryll's shoulder.

"Ouch, she put her foot in her mouth. But T, you gotta understand she was hurt last night, and when we are hurt we can sometimes say things we don't mean. You have never had this issue when you were dating, as far as I know." Brandon went to the refrigerator to grab the bagels and cream cheese, then to the drawer for a knife.

"True, but B, that's just not the route to go with me, I don't care how mad you are. That's a soft spot for me still and I know I do my best everyday not to end up like Dad."

"You aren't going to." Brandon assured his brother. Brandon grabbed the coffeepot and poured Taryll and himself a cup. As they sat at the kitchen table sipping coffee and eating bagels they talked about the night before. Brandon told Taryll he was just as wrong as Justice for what was said and done. Taryll didn't want to hear it, he was still pissed. Brandon told him he needed to start getting ready for work, and that he suggested Taryll fix it with his wife because he was not staying with him again tonight.

"Aww man, come on just one more night. I am not ready to head home just yet. I cannot go back as mad as I am. I don't want to say anything to J that I will regret later." Taryll said as Brandon walked toward his bedroom.

"Nah bro, BJ is spending the weekend with Sharon's parents, and me and the missus are going to enjoy every minute that he is gone. You gots to go too." Brandon threw over his shoulder.

Taryll finished his coffee and put his cup in the sink. He went back to the living room put his Tims on along with his polo shirt and grabbed his keys and wallet from the coffee table.

Chapter 24

Where is she?

Taryll, not ready to head home, headed back to his studio. He knew there were some tracks he could put together as well as edit the new tracks Too Real had record the week before. He also had a couple hours to kill before meeting with Mike and Gage from the private security company. Taryll pulled out into traffic and his phone rang, it was Rain.

"Hello." Taryll said when he answered the phone.

"I wanted to apologize for my behavior last night. Taryll, I find you irresistibly attractive. We were working on that song and all I could think about was you and me together. I didn't mean to cause any trouble for you with your wife." Rain said as she leaned against the wall in her apartment.

She had gone home and thought about what had happened, and at first, she didn't care about Justice and her feelings, but then she thought about if the roles were reversed. How would she feel if another woman was kissing on her husband?

Taryll was silent for a second then answered,

"Rain, we can no longer work together. I should have never allowed myself to be in the position we were in last night. I am not available, I am married… happily married. I forgive you for last night, but I am going to assign you to one of the other producers on my team."

Stephanie Tennile

Rain was quiet for a moment, and then stated she understood and would wait to hear from the other producer.

Taryll hung up the phone dropping it in the cup holder. He pulled up in front of his studio and parked in his spot. He sat there for a minute, thinking about everything that had transpired, and what he had told Rain. Happily married, he thought. He was happy, even with their first real argument as a married couple, he was still happy. Taryll jumped out of his truck and headed into the studio.

He had worked on some tracks, and then headed to the meeting with the bodyguards. Taryll was happy with the way the meeting went, and as he walked to his truck, he got Juan on the phone.

"Hey Juan." Taryll said as he unlocked his truck.

"Hey Taryll, how are you? How did the meeting go with Mike and Gage? Did you make your decision on which you wanted to hire to protect your wife?" Juan asked.

"Yes, I want to hire them both." Taryll said.

"Are you sure you need both Gage and Mike? I think hiring one or the other will be enough. You stated she was getting harassing phone calls, and you believe someone might be stalking her."

Taryll started his truck and switched to his Bluetooth. "That's right. I just want to ensure she's safe Juan."

"Taryll, from what you told me about the security system you have on your home, you have a good starting point. I would suggest you allow my company to install cameras on the property. Also, I would suggest you invest in having a security guard on site at her dance studios and the lot. But I think you only need Mike or Gage to be her personal bodyguard. From what you told me about your wife, she may not be happy with having someone following her around."

"Juan you're right. I think Gage might be the better fit. When can he start and when can you come and install the cameras?"

Juan told him Gage could start in the morning and he would get with the technicians and find out when their next available appointment was to have the cameras installed.

Taryll headed back to the studio to get with Bryce and Craig to go over the schedule for the upcoming week, as well as to let Craig know that he would be producing all of Rain's music moving forward. As he rushed into the studio, he left his cell phone in the cupholder in his truck.

As the day wore on his anger subsided. Justice was hurt by what happened, if it were the other way around, he would have gone through the roof. He finished up the track he was working on and turned off his equipment. It was getting late, and he still needed to talk to Justice about Gage starting as her bodyguard in the morning. He was going to call her and have the conversation but figured he should talk to her face to face about everything.

He stood up and he heard his stomach growl, he hadn't eaten since that morning, and it was just a bagel and coffee. If he left now, he would be able to catch their favorite Thai restaurant before they closed, then head home and have a conversation with Justice over dinner.

Justice woke up and it was completely dark all around her, and she was moving. She calmed her breathing and tried to adjust her eyes to the darkness around her. She realized she was in the trunk of a car. She couldn't move her arms or legs; her legs were tied together at the ankle and her wrists were bound behind her back. Her arms hurt from being tied behind her for so long. How long have I been tied up, she thought?

She wanted to yell but she knew she wouldn't be heard from the trunk of a moving car. She tried to adjust the way she was laying so she would get off her aching arms, but they hit a bump causing her to hit her head on the trunk knocking her out again.

Taryll grabbed his order and left the restaurant, heading home. His cell phone was dead because he had left it in the truck all day. When he got home, he unlocked the front door, and the alarm didn't go off. He took a deep breath and tried to relax. How many times do I have to tell her to set the damn alarm, he thought?

"Justice, babe, you need to remember to set the alarm." He said as he turned on the light in the living room. He walked into the kitchen and sat the food on the counter, she wasn't there. He went to the office, her computer was on, email open, and her glasses sat on the keyboard. Taryll took his jacket off and hung it in the closet; then headed to the bedroom. Their door was closed. It's early for her to be sleep, he thought. When Taryll opened the door, he saw Justice's cell phone smashed on the floor and the patio door open.

He started to panic, grabbing his cell phone out of his pocket he plugged it into the charger by their bed. He quickly turned his phone on and saw that he had two voicemail messages from Justice and a bunch of text messages. Oh no, he thought. He called his voicemail and put the phone on speaker.

"First message sent October 5th at 7:14am: 'Tar, it's me. Baby I'm so sorry for what I said last night. Please call me.' To save press 4, to delete press 7 to skip press 9." Taryll pressed 9 and the next message started to play.

"Next message sent October 5th at 5:16pm: 'Baby, it is five fifteen in the evening. I am worried, where are you?'" Taryll listened to the message then there was a voice in the background, but he couldn't make out what was being said and then he heard it, "Baby help me," and then he heard a scream muffled and the line went dead.

Taryll grabbed the house phone from Justice's side of the bed and called the police. He was afraid, mad, and determined to get his wife back.

Chapter 25
The Search Begins

Taryll was sitting at the dining room table answering the questions the police officers and detectives were asking him when Leslie walked into the house. He shook his head and answered the officer's question, but she couldn't make out what he was saying.

"Taryll, what happened?" She asked as she went to him. Taryll stood and held his mother-in-law in his arms.

"Someone kidnapped Justice." He stated, not believing the words coming from his mouth. He had just seen her last night.

He sounded so defeated. Leslie was shocked. Who would take her daughter, why would they take her?

"When why?" Leslie asked. Taryll looked at her and he was at a loss for words. He didn't know what was going on. He had hired the bodyguard and requested that cameras be installed around the house, her studios, and the lot, but Gage didn't start until the morning and the installation of the cameras couldn't happen until next week. He blamed himself, if he had just come home last night, or even this afternoon, maybe she would be here. He couldn't forgive himself for not being home.

Taryll sat at the table and watched as the detective dusted the house for prints and look for anything that would tell them who took Justice. Taryll didn't think they would find anything, if this was the same man who broke into their house when they first moved in, they wouldn't find anything because they didn't find any trace of him that night.

"Sir, you said you stayed with your brother last night, correct?" Detective Janessa Vaughn asked.

Janessa Vaughn was a twenty-six-year-old senior detective, ahead of her time. Other cops her age were still working the street not doing detective work. She usually worked homicide, but her captain specifically put her on this case. Everyone in Los Angeles knew Justice and Taryll Johnson. He had warned her when she left the department, not to mess this up.

"Yes, Ma'am I did. I was working late at the studio and his house is closer to the studio than mine, so I crashed on his sofa." Taryll said. It wasn't exactly a lie; he was tired when he left the studio, but he was also emotional drained and didn't want to deal with Justice and the fight they had.

"Can we listen to the message again Sir?" Taryll handed his cell phone to the detective, and she played the message on speaker. As she and her partner, Timothy Stanley, listened to it Timothy asked,

"Sir why would your wife be worried, did you not tell her you were at your brother's?"

Taryll sighed and ran his hands through his curly hair and looked at the detective.

"We had a fight earlier that night. She came to the studio after she left her dance studio. When she walked in there was another woman sitting in my lap kissing me." He said, ashamed as to what had transpired.

Leslie looked at her son in law and slapped him on his shoulder.

"How could you?" She asked angrily.

"Mom, please, it isn't what you think. We were working on a project, and she was excited at how it turned out. Before I knew it, she had dropped down in my lap and kissed me. Before I had the chance to react Justice walked in the door. Please know that I would never hurt J, I love her." The detective made notes in his notebook and then continued. I wonder if he is involved, Tim thought.

"Do you think the woman you were with that night had something to do with this? Could she be involved in the kidnapping of your wife?" Janessa asked.

"No Ma'am I don't. She called me this morning to apologize for what had happened. But I do think the man who broke in a few weeks ago had something to do with this. I think he took Justice." Taryll looked over at his mother-in-law and she had a confused look on her face.

"What man Taryll?" She asked as she sat at the table. This was all beginning to be too much for her to handle. Leslie was hearing about this for the first time. Why didn't anyone tell me, she thought. She got up and started to pace. Leslie had dealt with a psycho coming after her daughter in high school. It was one of the boys in her class.

"Mom, we didn't want to tell you or my mother for that matter because we didn't want to scare you. The night I came home from the airport, Justice and I were in the shower when someone broke into the house. When we came out of the bathroom the patio doors in our bedroom were open and neither of us had opened them. We called the police, and I walked around the house to see if anyone was outside. While I was checking the house, she said she saw a man standing in the living room." Leslie stopped pacing and stared at her son in law. She wanted to slap the shit out of him, but she held her composure.

"Who is he, what did he look like? Did you tell the police?" Leslie was ringing her hands. All she could think about was her baby somewhere hurt, scared, fighting for her life.

"We don't know who he is. We called the police, and they came out to the house. When they got here whoever he was, was gone. They didn't find anything, and nothing was missing." Taryll got up and started to pace. He needed to find Justice and get her home where she was supposed to be. He had a bad feeling the man that was in their house was the man responsible for taking Justice.

Taryll stopped and looked at his mother-in-law, he had a thought of who the person could be, but it had been years since they heard from him. Brent Collins was a guy they knew in high school. He had a big crush on Justice, so big that Justice had to get a restraining order against him after he attacked her on the beach.

"Mom, you don't think it could be Brent, do you?" He asked as he sat back down at the table.

"Who's Brent?" Janessa asked as she wrote the name in her notebook.

Leslie thought about it for a moment and sat next to Taryll at the table. They had gotten a restraining order against him because of the attack, and he went to juvenile hall for his last year of high school, but after that they hadn't heard from him, that had been almost ten years ago.

"I don't know, I don't think he would go to such lengths after all these years. He didn't even call her after the incident in high school." Leslie said trying to convince herself, but she couldn't be sure. He was the first person she thought of when they said Justice had been kidnapped. Could he still have feelings for her after all these years, she thought, maybe the news of Justice getting married triggered something within him?

Again, Janessa asked who Brent was. Taryll explained who he was and what he had done when they were in high school. Janessa and her partner both felt it was unlikely, too much time had passed, and he hadn't made contact since the incident in high school. However, they agreed they would look into him.

"If this man hasn't tried to contact her over the last ten years, then I doubt it's him. We can look into him for now, but we won't make contact unless we find something that ties him to this."

The detectives asked for any information they had on Brent and then headed back to the precinct to start analyzing the evidence that had been collected. Taryll locked the door behind the officers and leaned against it. He didn't know what to do; he was lost. If I had been home, he thought, if I had hired the bodyguard sooner.

Leslie got up from her seat at the dining room table and walked over to her son-in-law. She was scared to think what her daughter was going through but right now she needed to be strong for her son in law. She could see the guilt written all over Taryll's face.

"Taryll, they will find her. Justice is strong, she can handle herself." Leslie looked up at Taryll trying to reassure him as she tried to reassure herself. She had already lost her son; she couldn't bear to bury another child.

Chapter 26
The Face in the Shadows

Justice woke up again, and she was in a dimly lit room. She looked around and it looked as though she was in a basement. Her arms were no longer bound together but her ankle was chained to a pipe protruding from the wall. There was hardly anything in the room except for a few boxes and a tattered sofa in a corner and a folding table with two chairs. Justice stood up and she felt like her legs were made of jelly and her head was pounding; she lowered herself back to the floor.

"I gave you a mild sedative. I can't have you trying to fight me, now can I? I know you've been taking Tae Kwan Do and kickboxing for years, you must be very skilled by now." A male voice said from the shadows.

"Who are you? What do you want from me?" She slurred. Justice sat on the floor trying to get her eyes to focus in the direction the voice had come from.

"There will be plenty of time to talk later. Right now, I just need you to sleep." The man said. Justice tried to stand again but her legs gave out, and then she was out again.

Stephanie Tennile

It had been over forty-eight hours since Taryll had last seen his wife, and thirty-six since she left him the voicemail. He had been back and forth from the police department and his mother in law's house. His mother was out of town but was on her way home because of the news. Taryll had been bombarded with media at the studio, the house, and the police department. They were even camped out at their beach house in Malibu. He needed a place where he could get away from it all.

Taryll pulled into his brother's driveway, and parked. He sat in his truck for a while as he thought about how he could have prevented this from happening. Gage was on payroll starting this morning and offered to be his bodyguard in the event that someone tried to come after him, but he declined. He told him as soon as he got Justice home, she was to never leave his sight.

As he sat there, the front door opened, and it was his older brother. Brandon walked out and over to the passenger side of the truck. Taryll unlocked the door and Brandon got in. They sat for a moment, not saying a word. Taryll looked as though he hadn't slept since finding out that Justice was missing. There were bags under his eyes, and he hadn't shaved in at least two days.

"How you holdin' up? By the time you called me to tell me what happened, it was all over the news, social media, and the internet. I'm sorry Bro." Brandon said. He watched as his brother stared out the windshield.

Seizing Justice

"Brandon, if I had just gone home the other night, she would be here man. I could have prevented this, this... this is my fault. I was supposed to protect her B." Taryll said as he slammed his hand against the steering wheel.

"Don't do that, Tar. This ain't your fault. You couldn't have known something like this would happen, no one plans for something like this." Brandon said as Taryll pulled out the driveway.

"I should have hired the bodyguard sooner, like I wanted to B. We get recognized whenever we leave the house, especially Justice with all of the work she does with these artists. Then J never sets the alarm on the house and that is how he got back in. This is on me, I am her husband, I vowed to protect her, and now she is only God knows where, with God knows who, dealing with..." He couldn't finish his statement. He didn't want to think about what could be happening to her.

Taryll got onto the freeway and headed toward the beach. He knew that that was the one place he could go to clear his head. He and Justice would go to the beach a lot just to get away from everything that was happening around them. Taryll and Brandon rode in silence until they got to Venice Beach. Taryll parked his truck outside of Rick's Surf and Turf.

"Okay, I didn't know we were going to eat." Brandon said jokingly as he got out the truck. "Had I known I wouldn't have had dinner at the house. But I can always go for a Corona!" Brandon tried to lighten the mood.

"Sorry Man, you know how I am, I get nervous, I eat." He said as he walked into the restaurant. Taryll needed something that he could control and right now it was an order of fish tacos and possibly a six pack of Corona.

Justice woke up and really needed to relieve herself. She stood up and her legs didn't feel like jelly anymore and her head didn't hurt as bad. She reached up to feel the spot where she had hit her head in the trunk and winced. She had a gash on her forehead, but it had been cleaned and a bandage had been applied. She looked around; she was still in the dark basement. She looked for a window, but there wasn't one. She couldn't tell if it were day or night, or how long she had been there.

"Hello? Anyone there?" She called out hoarsely. She really had to use the restroom and couldn't hold it. "I need to use the restroom. Please can you hear me?"

"There is enough slack in the chain for you to get to the bathroom, there it is to your left." The man called and then she heard a door slam. Justice moved to her left and found a door. There was a small bathroom, with a sink and a toilet, neither looked as though it had been cleaned in a while. Justice relieved herself and then washed her hands. When she came back into the room, the man was sitting on the sofa in the shadows; she couldn't see his face. Justice stayed as far from him as the chain would allow. As she moved, she watched him stand up.

"I told you I won't hurt you so why are you running from me?" He asked as he walked over to her. Justice moved back toward the wall. There was no way she would be able to fight him in the condition she was in, he made sure of that.

Seizing Justice

Although the sedative had worn off, she wasn't at a hundred percent, more like at sixty, if she was honest with herself, it was more of a forty if she considered the circumstances. If she were to fight him and knock him out she was still chained to the wall with no way of getting away.

"Who are you?" She asked as she tried to see his face. He stayed in the shadows and just out of her reach. If he got to close, he knew she would try to attack him, and the last thing he wanted to do was hurt her, but he would if she tried.

"I'm surprised you don't remember who I am. You did send me to juvie." He said.

Justice didn't know what he was talking about. She hadn't sent anyone to juvie. She started at the figure that was looming in the shadows, and then he inched into the light. Justice gasped; it was Brent. He looked the same as he did in high school, except he was bigger in build than back then. His blue eyes were crystal clear and filled with hurt, just as she remembered. Even if she tried to fight her way out, he would be able to overpower her easily. Justice started to move, trying to put some distance between them, but she had no place to go.

"You remember me." Brent said with a smile, he knew she would as soon as she saw his face up close, this was why he had waited so long.

"You know, all I wanted was to take you to the Fall Ball. But because of you lying to me…"

"I didn't lie to..." Justice started.

"Shut up! I'm talking!" He shouted, causing Justice to jump. He inched toward Justice getting closer to her. When he realized, she wasn't going to fight he got right in her face, his blue eyes glowing with anger.

"You ruined my life. I spent the rest of my senior year in Juvenile Hall, had to get my GED, and lost my football scholarship to UCLA. Do you have any idea, what you did? You had your happily ever after. Graduated, went to Chapman University, and started your company, have worked with many recording artists and dance crews, married your high school sweetheart, and what did I get, a job as a janitor, working at different hotels." Brent yelled. He grabbed her arms, tightening his grip as he spoke.

"Please, I didn't know. I was told you transferred to another school." Justice said barely above a whisper. Brent stared at her and paused, the look in her eyes made him believe she was telling the truth. Maybe she didn't know, he thought.

"But in all you did, I still love you, Justice. I have never loved anyone else." He kissed her cheek and her neck. Justice struggled in his grip, trying to get away.

"Get off of me." She screamed as she tried to push him away. Brent tightened his grip, throwing her down and pinning her against the mattress.

"You are mine, forever. No one will ever find you." He whispered in her ear, as he put her in a choke hold. Justice tried to fight, but it was no use, he was too strong, she passed out. Brent got up and walked toward the stairs that lead up to the main floor. He would have her as his own. He stopped at the top of the stairs. He didn't want to hurt her, but she pushed him to it. He unlocked the door and slammed it behind him.

Chapter 27
The Call

Taryll got home as the sun was going down. He hadn't heard from the police department since that morning when they told him to go home. Thankfully the media had left; he guessed they were tired of camping out on his front lawn for a story they were never going to get. The media was already running their own version of what was going on, and some even thought he had something to do with Justice's disappearance. As he walked up to the house, his cell phone rang.

"Hello?" He answered.

"Hello Taryll." The distorted voice on the line said. Taryll stopped dead in his tracks.

"Who are you? Where's my wife?" He asked.

"She's with me, where she's supposed to be. You don't deserve her and the fact you were with another woman the night I came for her, well that just goes to show I'm right."

Taryll was mad, not only did he have his wife, but he had been watching them, this was the same man who broke into their house.

"What do you want?" Taryll asked.

"I have what I want… Justice." The man stated and then the line went dead. Taryll turned around and headed back to his truck. He had to get to the police station to see if they could trace the call.

Taryll pulled into the parking lot at the police department as Detective Vaughn was walking out. Taryll jumped out to catch her.

"Detective, Detective." He called as he jogged over to her car.

"Mr. Johnson, we haven't got anything new, please go home and get some rest. We are doing everything we can." She stated. She knew he wanted answers, but now they just didn't have anything.

This guy was good. He didn't leave any prints, fibers, hairs, anything that could tie him to the scene. She also knew if they didn't find her alive within the first 48 hours, there was a greater probability they would find her dead or wouldn't find her at all. That was the information she didn't want to give Mr. Johnson, it was the information she hated giving any family, it was one of the reasons she hated working kidnapping cases.

"No wait, he called. Please. It has to be Brent; it has to be." Taryll said. Janessa stopped walking and turned to Taryll.

"He called? You heard his voice?" She asked as she walked toward him.

"No Ma'am, it was distorted, but I know it was a man, because he said Justice was meant to be with him."

"Which number did he call, the house, your cell?" She started to walk back toward the precinct and Taryll followed close behind telling her about the call to his cell phone and what the man had said.

Seizing Justice

When they got inside Janessa asked for Taryll's cell phone and took it to the lab to see if the call could be traced back to its origin. As they waited to hear back, Janessa got Taryll a cup of coffee.

"Sir, from what you are telling me, and I don't mean to sound insensitive, he has what he wants. The only reason he would call, and I am being honest, is to taunt you. He hasn't asked for anything else." Janessa took a sip of her coffee. She hated to be so blunt, but what could she or anyone do. The kidnapper stated he had what he wanted, he wanted Justice and he had her.

"I know. But I also know my wife; she isn't going to let any man think she's his or has control over her and that scares me. She isn't even going to play along to prolong her life." Taryll looked down at his coffee and swallowed. Baby please, he thought, just play along until I can find you.

"Do you think she can get him to contact you again?" She asked.

"I don't know." Taryll said.

A technician walked into the break room and signaled for Janessa to come into the hallway. Taryll looked up and the look on the tech's face wasn't reassuring. He knew they were unable to trace the call.

"Mr. Johnson, the call was from a disposable cell phone, we're unable to trace it." Janessa said as she handed him back his cell phone. Taryll couldn't take it anymore; he went to throw his phone against the wall when it rang.

"Hello." Taryll said quickly.

"Tell me, what did the detective tell you?" The distorted voice asked. Taryll mouthed that it was the man. Janessa mouthed speaker, and Taryll turned it on.

"The call was untraceable." Taryll said. "Let me talk to Justice. I want to know she's alright." Taryll declared.

"Wow, no you have no upper hand here, you have no room to be making demands." The voice stated then laughed. "But like I told her, I won't hurt her, I love her. I have always loved her and always will."

"What do you want from me?" Taryll asked.

"I called because someone needs to tell you something." The voice stated and then there was a pause.

"Taryll..." Justice said groggily.

"Justice are you okay? Do you know where you are? Are you hurt?" He asked.

"Tell him!" He heard the voice in the background shout. Justice laid on the floor refusing to say what he wanted. "Tell him!" He yelled again as he kicked the wall by her head. Justice didn't flinch, she couldn't move.

"I... I... want to stay... here." She slurred. She was drugged. "We need... one million... dollars." She cried. Justice was laying on the floor next to the wall, the man hovering over her. She felt so heavy, she could barely move, all she could do was cry.

"Justice I am going to find you, baby, you hear me."

"Taryll, please hel..." She cried, and then he heard her scream.

"Justice..." Taryll yelled.

"Oh, now see you got her in trouble. I will call you with the location to drop off our money." The voice said.

"If you hurt her... I will kill you." Taryll said through clenched teeth.

"Hello... hello." The line had gone dead. Taryll slammed his fist into the table.

Janessa looked to the technician who was trying to trace the call; and he shook his head, nothing. She sat at the table and asked Taryll to sit. She had to figure out their next move.

"Do you have that type of money? The million dollars he's asking for?" She asked.

Taryll looked at her and nodded; with the sale of Justice's condo recently, there was that plus some in the savings account, but he was sure the man holding Justice knew that. He and Janessa worked out a plan to call the bank in the morning to schedule a pickup for the amount.

"This is what we will do." Janessa started. "When you go to pick it up, I will give you trackers to place in the bags with the money. We know now that he's watching you; you need to be very careful from here on out. He didn't say to keep the police out of it, but I am sure he wouldn't want us following you to the location of the drop when he gives it to you. With that being said, we will have an officer within reach of you at all times. You will not know who he or she is, so you don't blow their cover, to ensure your wife is as safe as possible."

Taryll nodded and let her continue. She told him they would go ahead and tap his cell phone and house phone, so they would know when and where the drop was without him having to inform them or be seen with another cop.

"Because this man already knows who I am, I will not see you again until we get your wife back. Do you have any questions?"

"I want her back safe. I am willing to do anything to get her back."

Taryll's phone rang, it was his mother she was parked outside of his house.

Justice leaned over the toilet dry heaving. Her body wanted to throw up but there was nothing in her stomach. She couldn't remember the last time she had eaten. She went to the sink and splashed water on her face. She was shaking, and couldn't focus, whatever he had injected her with the last time wasn't wearing off like before. She looked at her face in the mirror and splashed her face with water again. Then all of a sudden, she felt sick again.

As she leaned back over the toilet the thought of the baby came back to her mind. I can't be pregnant, she thought. Her head was throbbing, she felt as though she had a hangover. Justice leaned back against the dirty tile wall behind her and took deep breaths.

"Justice?" Brent called as he came down the stairs.

Justice closed the bathroom door as the tears started to run down her face. She wanted to go home, but she knew he would never let her go; once Brent got the money, he asked for he intended to run with her in tow. This wasn't going to end well.

"Justice, I called you." Brent yelled, causing Justice to jump. He said he wouldn't hurt her, but she wasn't sure. He yelled at her a lot and slammed doors. She hated it. She couldn't fight back, whatever he was using to keep her compliant was keeping her from focusing and weak, and he was too strong.

"I'm in the bathroom. What did you give me?" She said faintly. She turned the water on at the sink and splashed her face again. She could feel herself getting tired again, she had to stay awake, and she had to fight the drug that was in her system if she was going to survive.

Brent banged on the door. She had been in the bathroom most of the day and he was starting to get scared that he may have over drugged her.

"Justice, I brought you something to eat. Please come out." Brent said ignoring her question. He thought about the last injection he gave her; he had done it over eight hours ago, the sedative should have worn off by now.

Justice got up from the floor and opened the bathroom door. She looked up at Brent as he backed away to allow her room to come out. He sat the food on the table; from the smell coming from the bags, it seemed to be Mexican. Justice inched toward the table, not because she was hesitant, but because of how heavy her body felt. Brent pulled the chair out for her, and Justice sat.

"I didn't know what you wanted so I got tacos, burritos, salsa and chips." He said.

Does he really think we're old friends having dinner, she thought? Justice didn't say anything; she just waited to see what he was going to do. Brent sat a couple of carne asada tacos in front of Justice and waited for her to start eating. Justice unwrapped one of the tacos and took a small bite. She was so hungry, but she could not run the risk of making herself sick by eating too fast.

As she took small bites, Brent watched her eat. He was getting upset with himself because this wasn't the woman he wanted. She had been with him for the last five days and she had been out of it for the majority of it. He didn't want to have to drug her to make her comply with his requests, but he knew from all the years he had been watching Justice she wasn't going to be easily handled.

He knew of her black belt in Tae Kwan Do, the fact she started taking Krav Maga, and he knew she worked out every morning like clockwork. He had been doing his share of working out, but he wasn't as skilled in martial arts as she was; and even if he was, the last thing he wanted to do was hurt her.

"Why do I still feel like this?" Justice asked. She looked Brent in his face, trying to show him that she wasn't afraid of him.

"The sedative is taking longer to wear off because I gave you more prior to our phone call to Taryll." Brent said clenching his teeth at the mention of Taryll. He knew Justice loved him, but he would soon change that, she would love no other man but him.

"Why do you feel you have to drug me? I know I have a better chance at surviving if I comply, the drugs aren't necessary." She said slowly. Justice needed to gain his trust and she knew the only way to do it was to play into his fantasy. Justice stood and pulled her sweatshirt over her head, exposing her nude-colored camisole. She still had on her pajamas from when he grabbed her from her home. She put the sweatshirt on the back of the chair and sat back in her seat.

He wants me to be his, she thought, let's go ahead and play his game. Justice would do what she had to, to get home to her family.

Chapter 28

The Game

Justice finished her tacos and sighed. Let the games begin, she thought. She looked down at the shackle around her ankle and then grabbed a chip and dipped it in the salsa.

"What's wrong Justice?" Brent asked.

"I was just thinking; it is really hard to spend time with you if you are never down here, and I am shackled to a wall." She said and grabbed another chip. Justice was trying to be as casual as she could.

Brent looked at Justice and was skeptical. She hadn't said anything other than why had he taken her since she got here. Then he thought, she hasn't mentioned that man either, maybe there is trouble in paradise. Brent stood up and walked toward the stairs.

"Well, maybe later I can unshackle you and you can come up and watch a movie with me." He said as he started up the stairs.

"Can I have popcorn and Raisinets? They're my favorite." Justice asked with a smile. Brent smiled back and took the stairs two at a time. I have to go get her snacks, he thought.

Justice leaned back in the chair and was excited. She prayed she was getting to him, and he wasn't only dragging her along in a game of his own.

Later that evening Justice sat on the mattress on the floor in the basement. She was starting to think her plan hadn't worked. She hadn't heard anything from the floor above since Brent left her after he ate. By the way she felt it had to have been hours ago. She was starting to regain her strength and she was starting to get hungry again. Justice stood and walked over to the table. The bag with the Mexican food was still sitting on the table. She looked into the bag and there was one last taco. She took it out of the bag, unwrapped the taco and ate it in three bites. What she really wanted was an orange cream soda. She hadn't had a soda in years, but now she was really craving an orange cream soda.

She sat back down on the mattress and rubbed her ankle where the shackle was rubbing against it. It was sore, but she could stand the pain, it wasn't as bad as it could be. As she got up, she heard the door at the top of the stairs open. She watched as Brent came down the stairs and toward her. Neither of them said anything.

"I got a movie. I hope you like it." He said as he bent down to face her.

"Well I am sure whatever it is, has to be better than being down here in the dark."

Justice looked at him, trying to figure out what it was he was thinking. Justice rubbed her ankle as she looked him in the eye. She needed him to see just how uncomfortable she was in this shackle, but she also had to win his trust.

"There is something you need to do before we watch our movie." Brent said as he straightened up and walked over to the table. Justice didn't like the sound of that. The last time he told her she needed to do something, she had to call and ask Taryll for a million dollars.

"What?" She asked getting up as well.

"You need to call him and tell him where to leave the money." Brent said as he pulled his phone out of his pocket. It had been a long time since they talked about the money. It had to have been days since the first call, she thought.

"Where do you want him to leave it?" She asked making sure not to say Taryll's name. She had been doing really well up until the last time she was on the phone; when she had said his name, Brent got so upset he had kicked a hole in the wall next to where she was laying. She was afraid he would kick her, but he has made it very apparent he was not going to hurt her. Even with that being said, she still didn't want to push her luck with him; Brent had beat her up pretty bad when they were in high school.

"I want him to leave it at the park a few blocks from your studio. The park you run at sometimes." He said. Justice winced at the thought that he had been watching her as long as he had; she hadn't run in the park in over a year.

"What's wrong?" He asked raising his voice. Justice cursed to herself. Be mindful of your reactions, she thought. She didn't want to lose what little trust she thought she was building with him.

"My ankle, it hurts." She said quickly. She almost blew it. If she reacted contrary to what she wanted him to believe she would be sedated again, she knew it.

"The shackle is rubbing against my ankle bone." She added. Justice reached down to her ankle and rubbed above the shackle.

Brent paused and watched her. He still had a hard time trusting her. He wanted to, but he just didn't know. A person would do anything to regain their freedom. He grabbed his phone and dialed the number as he adjusted the voice modulator to disguise his voice.

Taryll was worried; it had been three days since the phone call from Justice, and five since she had gone missing. He knew he was going to have to talk to the man who took her again so he could drop off the money, but this man wasn't going to give her up. His intention was to run with her by his side.

He had talked to Juan at the security company, telling him what had happened. Juan had his technicians stop what they were working on and made Taryll the priority. He had his team install the cameras at their house in Los Angeles, and the beach house in Malibu.

He had also spoken to Gage about the money request. Gage felt he should do the hand off instead of Taryll, but Taryll was against the idea. He wanted to be there in the event Justice was there. He also didn't want to scare the guy off.

Taryll sat on the sofa in the living room contemplating what his wife could possibly be going through; did he really want to know? Taryll ran his hand through his hair and sighed.

"Taryll, it is going on two o'clock in the morning sweetheart, please go to bed." His mother said as she walked into the living room. She had been with him for the last three days and she couldn't remember a time he had actually slept.

"Mom, if I were here that night she wouldn't be gone." He said without looking up. Tears fell down his cheeks.

"Taryll you can't do this to yourself. The police are going to get her back." She said as she sat next to her son. Her heart hurt for him, she hated to see him in so much pain. During this whole ordeal she couldn't bring herself to think of Justice. She loved her like her own, and just the thought of Justice not being safe made her want to weep.

Taryll got up and went to his room, he needed to sleep but it just wouldn't come. Angela sat on the sofa and watched her son disappear down the hallway. She leaned back and cried silently. What happens if they don't get her back, she thought. She wiped her face and shook her head, I am not going to think like that, she thought. She got up and went to the kitchen to fix herself a cup of tea. If she was right Leslie, Justice's mother, would be up any minute as well.

Justice looked at the phone in Brent's hand. If I seem too eager to make this call, he'll know I am only playing with him, but if I ask him to wait maybe he'll believe me, she thought. Justice looked at Brent and shrugged.

"Can we watch our movie first?" She asked. Justice looked at him trying to gage his reaction.

"Really?" Brent asked skeptical.

"Really, I am bored and lonely down here. A couple of hours won't kill anyone, well maybe him, but who cares about that." She said trying to sound uncaring. She hated the fact she was going to cause her husband more pain by waiting a couple more hours.

"I can call after the movie."

Brent looked at her and she smiled at him. He took his keys out of his pocket and walked around to the other side of the table.

"Sit down." He ordered.

Justice did as he ordered and sat in the chair at the table. She watched as he unlocked the shackle around her ankle. Justice flexed her ankle and winced. It didn't hurt, it was just sore, but she needed him to think she was in pain. Justice put her foot on the floor and groaned.

"Are you alright J?" Brent asked.

Bingo, she thought. In high school he had never called her Justice, it was always J. The only time he called her Justice was when he attacked her on the beach. She had him right where she wanted him. Not once, since he had taken her had he called her J, he was starting to trust her and that was exactly what she needed to get back home to her family.

"I guess the shackle did a little more damage than I thought. It really hurts when I put weight on it. How long have I been shackled to the wall?" Justice brought her ankle up into her lap and started to massage it, making faces as she did to give the illusion that it was painful. Brent threw the shackle aside and sat back down at the table.

"You have been here for almost six days." He said looking at his phone again.

Justice was shocked; she couldn't believe she had been here that long. As she thought about the time, she realized a good part of it she had spent sedated. Justice wanted to strangle him, but she had to play along, she had to make him think she wanted to be with him. I have to get back to Taryll, she thought.

"Well what movie did you get?" She asked.

"Your favorite, *Gone in Sixty Seconds*." He said. He was right that was one of her favorite movies.

"Did you remember the..." she started.

"Raisinets and popcorn. It's upstairs waiting for you." He finished. He stood up and waited for Justice to stand.

This is my chance to play with his mind, she thought. Justice stood up from the table then allowed her knee to buckle.

He came to her side, catching her by the waist. Justice looked at him and winced again as she put her foot down.

"It hurts when I put pressure on it. I don't think I am going to make it up the stairs." She said. Brent got ready to say something and she interrupted.

"Could you carry me?" She asked looking up at him through her lashes. Brent lifted her in one fluid motion, without saying a word and carried her up the stairs. Being in his arms made her want to vomit, but Justice just kept thinking of her husband and getting back to him. I will do anything, endure anything to get back to you, she thought as Brent carried her up the stairs. To play with his mind, she nestled her head in the crook of his neck as he walked up the stairs. Anything, she thought, I will do anything to get home to you.

Chapter 29
The Drop

Justice sat on the sofa next to Brent trying really hard to pretend she was interested in the movie and not her surroundings. She would glance around a couple times then turn her focus back to the movie and make comments here and there to make him believe she was enjoying herself. All she wanted to do was to get out, but she had to figure out where she was.

As the movie came to an end Justice stretched her arms above her head and pretended to be tired. Brent got up to turn the movie off. Justice glanced over her shoulder toward the front door. She strained to see if the door was locked and judged would she be able to make it to the door and out before he could catch her.

It's too risky, she thought. If she didn't make it he would throw her back in the basement and she would have lost his trust and she would never get out, but if she made it she could run to a neighbor and call the police. Justice scooted to the edge of the sofa and was about to get up when Brent got up from his spot on the floor in front of the television where he was changing the DVDs.

"We have a phone call to make." He said as he came back to the sofa sitting next to her with his arm draped over the back of the sofa behind her. Justice looked at him, knowing what he was talking about. She nodded her head. Brent grabbed the phone and dialed Justice's house.

The phone rang twice before Leslie picked it up. "Hello?" She said quietly.

"Mom?" Justice said shocked. Her mother was there, tears started to run down her face. Brent grabbed the phone and told Justice to shut up. This was not a part of the plan. What is she doing there, he thought? Brent's face turned red, and he was getting pissed.

"Justice are you okay? Baby, where are you?" She asked in a panic as she waved Angela toward her and mouthed its Justice. Angela went to get Taryll. She ran down the hallway to Taryll's bedroom and opened the door.

"Justice is on the phone." She said. Taryll grabbed the phone from the nightstand and realized the phone battery was dead, that was why he hadn't heard the phone ring. He ran out of the room to the living room. Leslie was crying as she begged to talk to her daughter.

"I need to talk to him…now." Brent said into the voice modulator over the receiver. Leslie handed the phone to Taryll.

"Justice…" Taryll said into the receiver.

"Sorry, but she isn't coming to the phone. The drop will talk place at the park three blocks from J's studio. Be there in two hours." He said and then hung up the phone.

Taryll looked at the cordless phone in his hand then threw it across the room where it hit the wall breaking into pieces. Leslie jumped.

"Taryll baby, what did he say?" Leslie asked as she held onto Angela.

"The drop is in two hours at the park by J's studio. He didn't say anything else." He said as he headed to his room to change. He needed to ensure that he was there in time for the drop.

Justice sat on the sofa with tears in her eyes. She wasn't expecting her mother to answer the phone. She had prepared herself to hear the worry in her husband's voice but not her mother. Her mother was scared for her and she knew it. She was starting to doubt if she had the strength to fight back when the time came. Brent came back into the room and saw the tears in her eyes.

"Justice." He said. Justice quickly wiped the tears from her eyes and looked up at him.

"I wasn't expecting to talk to my mom." She answered honestly. She still needed him to think she was willing to run away with him. "But I'll be okay once we get away."

Brent looked at her skeptically as he handed her her shoes. He watched her as she put her shoes on. When she went to put her shoe on, she carefully put her shoe on her right foot that was the ankle that had been shackled to the wall for the last six days. Brent felt bad because he had hurt her. He didn't intend to hurt her; he just didn't want her to run. He looked at his watch and told her that it was time to go.

He helped her up from the sofa and walked her out of the house and to the car, where he opened the trunk.

"Get in." He said.

"What?" Justice asked shocked. She crossed her arms across her chest and didn't move.

"I can't take the risk of you trying to jump out the car."

Justice looked at him in amazement. Does he truly think I am going to ride in the trunk willingly, I almost hyperventilated on the way here, she thought.

"I am not stupid, why would I jump out of a moving car?" She said trying to sound as offended as she possibly could. She stood her ground.

Brent slammed the trunk causing Justice to jump. He opened the back door on the driver's side and told her to get in and stay down. Justice did as she was told. She sat on the floor of the car. As she sat there, she rotated her ankle trying to get past the pain. She needed to know that when the time came, she would be able to run.

Gage followed behind Taryll as he headed to the office to grab the suitcase with the money.

"Mr. Johnson, you should really consider letting me do the drop." He said.

"Gage, I have to be the one to do it. This guy is expecting me to bring the money. He needs to see my face; he needs to know that it is killing me that he has her. I have to play into his delusion."

Taryll grabbed the suitcase with the money in it and headed to the car he had to get to the drop site and somehow get Justice back. What if he doesn't bring her to the park, he thought as he put the case in the back of his Land Rover.

"At least tell me where the drop is, I can be there." Gage said as he watched Taryll put the suitcase in the truck.

"Gage stay here with my mother and mother-in-law please. I'll call you when it is over."

He climbed behind the wheel and pulled out the driveway. He looked in his rear-view mirror and noticed that about a block behind him was a car following him.

He prayed it was the police officer Janessa had told him about. But he also hoped he or she wasn't noticed by the man he spoke to. The last thing he needed was him getting suspicious if he wasn't already.

He got on the highway and headed toward Justice's studio. He was so nervous. As he got off at his exited, he passed the studio and headed to the park. He saw the car that was following him drive past the parking lot and keep going. Maybe that wasn't them, he thought, she did say I wouldn't know where they were, but they would be close enough to act. As he sat in the driver seat, he waited to be contacted again by the man who had his wife. He wanted to kill him, make him pay for the time he had her. Justice had been gone almost a week and he didn't know what her condition would be when he got her back.

Ten minutes passed and it was almost time to hand over the money. Taryll looked at his watch again for the second time in two minutes. His phone rang.

"Hello?" He answered on the first ring.

"You are going to get out and head toward the jungle gym. Leave the bag under the monkey bars." The man said and then the line went dead.

Taryll got out the truck and went to the back and got the suitcase. He couldn't see anyone out in the park or within walking distance of the playground. It was just him and the darkness. As he closed the door a homeless man pushing a shopping cart walked over to him.

"Would you be able to spare a couple of dollars so I can get a cup of coffee?" The man asked with his hand out. Taryll wanted to tell the man to get lost, but he reached in his pocket pulled out a ten-dollar bill and handed it to the man.

"Thank you, sir. Your help is here." The man said and flashed his badge as he put the ten in his pocket. Taryll sighed with relief as he picked up the case and headed toward the jungle gym. His phone rang, he sent the call to his Bluetooth.

"Who were you talking to?" The man asked in his distorted voice. Taryll looked around the park and didn't see anyone.

"A homeless man asked for a couple of dollars for some coffee. Where are you?" Taryll looked around.

"Don't worry about me. Leave the money and get back in your truck."

"No, I want to know she's alright. I want to see Justice." Taryll said.

There was a pause on the line and the man contemplated. How great would it be to see her take the money and walk out of his life, he thought? The pain in his eyes would be priceless.

"Fine you want to see her." He said then ended the call.

Brent pushed Justice toward the jungle gym as he walked behind her with a gun in her back.

"Don't you do anything stupid, or I will kill him and then you." Bent said.

"I thought you weren't going to hurt me?" She asked as she feigned a limp. Justice was pissed, she really wanted to run but knew she couldn't, due to her ankle and the fact he had a gun pressed to the small of her back.

"I don't want to, but don't push me. If I can't have you no one can." He said.

Taryll watched as they walked toward them. Justice was limping. She's hurt, he thought. He started to walk toward her.

"Stop where you are!" The man shouted. When they came into view, Taryll knew who it was, Brent

Collins. He could kill him. How, he thought? All these years and he still hadn't gotten over her.

"Brent! Let her go." Taryll shouted. He wanted to attack him, but he knew Brent was crazy. He would kill her if he pushed him to it.

"So, you do remember me!" Brent shouted back.

He pushed Justice forward toward the bag, telling her to grab it in the process. Justice tried lifting the bag off the ground and noticed how heavy it was. She would be able to lift it a little but not lift and carry. She had to do something. If Brent got the money, he would leave with her and there was the possibility she would never see her family again.

"I can't, it's too heavy." She said as she tried to lift it again.

"Drag it!" He shouted at her. Justice dragged the bag through the sand. She looked up at Taryll and winked at him. He mouthed no, but it was too late. Justice grabbed the bag with all the strength she had and swung it, hitting Brent's arm causing him to drop the gun. Justice fell to the ground with the bag and Taryll ran to grab the gun pointing it at Brent, but it was too late he had already grabbed Justice, as she tried to get up, he grabbed her by the hair pulling her up into his grasp. Justice pulled away and went to run when he pulled another gun from his waistband at the small of his back.

"You shouldn't have done that." Justice froze where she stood.

"Drop the gun Taryll or I'll shoot her where she stands." He said. Taryll dropped the gun. He backed up a little.

"Don't hurt her." Taryll said as Justice pleaded,

"Don't hurt him please."

"Shut up! You played me." Brent yelled. Justice inched toward Brent, and he cocked the gun.

"Don't come any closer Justice." He said. Justice was just as close as she needed to be.

"I don't want to hurt you." He said.

"You would never hurt me. You said so yourself." Justice said. Her heart was racing. When were the police going to come out from wherever they were, she thought? She knew her husband wouldn't have showed up alone.

"If I can't have you..." He said. Justice knew what he was going to do. He wasn't going to hurt her he was going to kill Taryll. She glanced over her shoulder and looked at her husband.

"No!" She yelled as she ran toward Taryll and then the gun went off.

Justice collapsed into her husband and there was a burning in her left shoulder.

"Justice." He said as he held her tight. He looked down at her and her eyes rolled to the back of her head. Then he heard two shots ring out from somewhere in the distance. When he looked up Brent was laying in the sand with two bullet holes in his chest.

"J, baby. Baby open your eyes. Look at me!" He said as he lifted her off her feet.

As the police and paramedics swarmed the scene, the paramedics took Justice out of his arms and laid her on the stretcher. They started to work on her as they pushed the stretcher back to the ambulance to take her to the hospital.

"What happened? Where were your men?" Taryll yelled as she saw Detective Vaughn jogging toward him.

"Mr. Johnson, we didn't have a clear shot of the kidnapper while your wife was in the way. I am sorry she was hurt in the process. The paramedic said she took a bullet to the shoulder. She should be fine. I would suggest you head to the hospital."

Taryll wanted to be mad at the detective, but they did get his wife back. Detective Vaughn told Taryll they would take the money to the precinct, and he could pick it up later. Taryll ran to his truck and drove to the hospital.

Chapter 30
The reunion

One the way to the hospital Taryll had called the house and Gage answered. He let him know they had gotten Justice and to bring their mothers to the hospital. He then called his brother and updated him on what had transpired. He was pissed Justice put herself at risk the way she did; but then he knew the woman he married. She wasn't the type not to fight back.

When he got to the hospital's emergency room, he was told Justice was in surgery to have the bullet removed from her shoulder and she would be put in a private room afterward for recovery. Taryll sat in the waiting room praying there would be no complications and she would be alright.

"Taryll where is she?" Leslie said as she came running in with Angela.

"She's in surgery to have a bullet removed from her shoulder. Brent was going to kill me, and she got in the way of the bullet." He said as he hugged his mother-in-law and then his mother. He sat them down and explained what had taken place. As he was explaining how she had gotten shot, Brandon walked into the hospital with his wife and their son.

Taryll stood up and hugged his brother and sister-in-law. Brandon looked at his younger brother. The whole ordeal had aged his brother. He looked so tired and worn down.

"How is she Tar?" Brandon asked.

"Not good man, J took a bullet for me. She's in surgery now." He said as he flopped back into the seat he was sitting in between his mother and mother-in-law. His mother continued to rub his back and tried her best to comfort him, but she knew he wouldn't be alright until he heard from the doctor.

They sat in the waiting room for another hour before the doctor finally came to speak with them.

"Mr. Johnson?" He asked as he came into the waiting room.

"Yes, that's me." Taryll said as he got up from his seat to meet with the doctor.

"Your wife pulled through surgery very well. She and the babies will be just fine." He said as he shook Taryll's hand.

"Babies!?!" Taryll almost passed out himself.

"Yes, your wife is almost three months pregnant."

Taryll looked at the doctor and then thought about the time he had spoken to her on the phone, and she sounded as though she had been drugged with something.

"She was sedated with something while she was being held. Did the drug she was given effect the babies in anyway?" Taryll asked.

"We did some bloodwork. Whatever she was sedated with wasn't in her system when she got here, but we can monitor her and the babies. Right now, it's too early to tell. We did an ultrasound, and the fetal heartbeats are very strong. We can run some test later in her pregnancy to make sure there was no damage done." The doctor stated and then walked off.

Taryll walked back over to his waiting family and sat back down.

"Tar man, what's wrong? Is Justice alright? Did she pull through?" Brandon asked as he sat next to his brother. Taryll had a lost look plastered on his face. Pregnant, he thought.

"She's fine... she's pregnant." He said. Taryll was in a daze. He could have lost his wife and his unborn children.

"She's pregnant." He muttered and then he started to cry. Brandon patted him on the back and congratulated him. Taryll was in shock. Pregnant, he thought over and over.

Angela hugged Leslie and they both wept. They were going to be grandmothers. Angela went to the desk to speak with the nurse about Justice's prenatal test to ensure that the baby was in fact healthy. Everything in her charts stated the babies were healthy but more tests would have to be done later in her pregnancy to ensure no long-term damage was done due to Justice being sedated over the last week. As Angela was talking with the nurse, the nurse received call saying Justice was in recovery and her family could go ahead and see her now.

Taryll was the first to walk in and when he saw his wife, he quietly walked over to her bed side. This wasn't the first time he had to see her lying in a hospital bed and he hated it. He sat on the edge of her bed and stroked her cheek. Justice jumped and her eyes popped open.

"It's me babe, calm down, it's just me." Taryll said and he could feel her relax under his touch.

"I thought I would never see you again." She said as tears started to run down her face. She looked at her husband, he was drained. He hadn't shaved in days and there were dark circles under his eyes.

"When was the last time you slept?" She asked as she touched his cheek. She cried softly, it hurt her to see her husband this way. She missed him so much.

"I couldn't sleep knowing you were somewhere possibly hurt or worst." He said. He looked at his wife and cringed at what he was thinking. He knew he would have to ask because the police would ask her too.

"Did he..." he started but couldn't get it out. If he touched her, he wouldn't forgive himself.

"No. No, he didn't touch me." She said, inwardly thanking God he hadn't. She looked Taryll directly in his eyes to assure him.

"I'm sorry baby, I am so sorry. I should have set the alarm… and….and told you sooner…I…" She said as she cried.

"What? No, Justice this isn't your fault." He kissed her forehead. "You didn't do this, it was him. This is not your fault, okay?"

Justice nodded her head and wiped away her tears with the back of her hand.

"Where are our moms?" She asked as she looked around him to the door.

"They are waiting in the waiting room. I wanted to talk to you first. There is something that I don't think you know." He said.

"Okay." Justice looked at her husband and his facial expression changed.

"You're pregnant." He said with a smile.

Justice looked at him and smiled. So, the feelings she was having, the sickness, the cravings, were all because she was pregnant. The vision she had was for her.

"I felt like I was, but I wasn't sure. It was when I was locked away that I truly thought I was." She said and then a look of fear came across her face. "I was sedated for most of the time I was gone. Is the baby, okay? Did the sedative he gave me hurt our baby?" She panicked as she placed her hand over her abdomen. Taryll placed his hand over the top of hers.

"According to the doctor the *babies* are healthy and have strong heartbeats. He said there are some tests he can do later in your pregnancy to ensure there was no permanent damage done."

"Babies?" she asked, Taryll nodded.

Justice nodded and closed her eyes. She was tired and all she wanted to do was sleep. She was safe now, and so was her husband and that was all that she cared about.

"Brent?" She asked.

"He was killed at the scene." He said. Justice nodded and closed her eyes. She could sleep, it was over, Brent was gone for good. Taryll got up and walked out to the waiting room where the rest of their family was waiting for an update. He let them know she was okay, and she was resting.

Brandon offered to drive his mother home and she declined stating she wanted to head home with Leslie, so she wasn't alone tonight. He lifted his son out of the chair to carry him to the car as his wife said good night to everyone.

As Leslie hugged everyone good night, then told Taryll that she wanted to see her daughter. Angela held her hand as they walked down the hall to her room. When they opened the door, Justice was sleeping. Leslie went over and kissed her on the forehead and told Taryll that she would be back in the morning.

Taryll walked his mother and mother-in-law back out to the waiting room where Gage was still waiting. Taryll asked that he drive them to Leslie's home, and then he could go home for the night. Gage nodded and told Taryll he would see him tomorrow morning.

They promised to call when they got in and told him to get some rest. As he watched them drive off, he waved goodbye and then headed back to Justice's room.

When he made it back up to the sixth floor, Detective Vaughn was waiting in the waiting room. Taryll walked over to her and shook her hand.

"I am sorry for yelling at you earlier." Taryll said before she had the chance to speak. "That was wrong of me. You're the reason my wife and myself are alive in the first place and for that, thank you."

Detective Vaughn asked him to have a seat in the waiting area.

"Sir, I am happy we got your wife back safe. I am sorry she was injured in the process. When we scooped out the location, we thought the drop was going to be made in the parking lot and that was where we were set up. We had no reason to think he would pull you into the park. When he told you to move to the playground, we knew we wouldn't have a great vantage point and I think that was what he was counting on." Detective Vaughn said as she sat in the seat across from Taryll in the waiting room. Taryll nodded and she continued.

"Your money is in the evidence locker at the precinct. We have removed all tracking devices so whenever you want you can come and pick it up all you have to do is sign the release forms." Janessa stood and Taryll followed her motion.

"Thank you. For all you've done. I appreciate all of your help." Taryll stuck his hand out and she took it. She was happy it ended as well as it did. She truly thought it would have ended much differently.

"Your wife is a brave woman. We could use someone like her on the force." Janessa said with a smile.

"Thank you, but this is the last time she is going to be in a situation like this." He smiled.

Chapter 31

Six Months later

"Push Justice, push!" Doctor Sanchez urged from his seat at the end of the delivery table.

"I can't...I can't. I can't push anymore." Justice breathed. She had been in labor for the last seventeen hours and she just didn't have any more energy. She had already given birth to the first baby, a little boy, and now she was drained. She felt as though her body was going to rip in half. Taryll was standing at her side coaching her through.

"Baby you can do this." He said. Justice could feel the tears running down her face, she couldn't push anymore. She was so tired.

"Justice one more good push." Doctor Sanchez called out.

With everything she had in her she pushed, and it was over. She could hear the cries of her baby.

"It's a boy." Doctor Sanchez said. "Dad, would you like to cut the cord?"

Taryll went and took the scissors from the nurse and cut the cord. He watched as they cleaned up his son. They handed the little boy to him, and he froze where he stood. He was so small, but so very loud nothing like his older brother. He looked at him and smiled.

"It's okay man, hold on. I know what you need." Taryll took their son to Justice. As he handed him to her, he stopped crying and stared at her.

"There there, you're alright." She said. Taryll kissed her forehead and then their son.

"You did it." He whispered in Justice's ear. Justice smiled at her husband and looked back at her son. She didn't know she could love someone so much.

"Okay, we need a name for his birth certificate." The nursed stated.

"Taryll Greyson Johnson Junior." Justice said with a smile as she looked up at her husband. Taryll smiled and kissed her again.

Taryll whispered he would be back with their mother's. Justice looked down at her son who was now sleeping soundly in her arms.

"Ma'am would you like me to take him?" The nurse asked.

"No, thank you. I just want to hold him." Justice sat in the bed holding her son brushing her finger over his beautiful head of hair. There was a crib next to her bed where her eldest son, Justin Ryan Johnson, by twelve minutes, lay sleeping. They were the most beautiful things she had ever done.

"I love you Greyson. Your mommy loves you so much." Justice said as she heard the door open. Her mother and mother-in-law walked into the room and smiled.

"Oh, Justice they're beautiful." Angela said as she kissed the top of his head.

"My baby is a mommy." Leslie said as she kissed Justice on the cheek. Justice smiled.

"What's his name?" Angela asked.

"Taryll Greyson Johnson Junior. I named him after his father, but I'll call him Greyson, so I don't confuse my husband. The little man over there, that's Justin Ryan Johnson." She said with a smile. She had named him after her brother.

Greyson started to squirm then he started to cry. Justice looked down at him and tried to comfort him, but he continued to cry.

"Mom?" Justice said in a panic.

"Don't worry baby, he's just hungry." Leslie said. The nurse came into the room to help Justice feed Greyson for the first time. As she nursed her son, she watched him and smiled. She knew she would have her hands full with two little ones, but she couldn't be happier.

Justin started to whine, and Taryll got up from his seat on the end of the bed and grabbed him out of the crib. As he rocked him, he stopped whining and went back to sleep.

"Your brother is going to be a handful, and you are more laid back huh Justin?" Taryll whispered to his son.

Justice looked up at her husband as he rocked Justin. She smiled as the tears started to run down her cheeks. She had everything she had ever wanted. She married the man she had loved since childhood, a beautiful family, and her dream career. Justice couldn't ask for anything else. She was truly blessed and filled with joy.

Seizing Justice

Stephanie Tennile

Made in the USA
Coppell, TX
18 January 2026

69486569R00105